"In spite of the cold, it's a lovely evening to go caroling, isn't it?"

The thick snow obscured the horizon and made it feel as if they were riding inside a glass snow globe. The twins tried to catch snowflakes on their tongues between giggles.

Their first destination was only a mile from John's house. As Lucy and Megan scrambled down from the sleigh, John offered Willa his hand to help her out. When she took it, he gave her an affectionate squeeze. She graced him with a shy smile in return.

"Was this what you imagined Christmas would be like when you decided to return to your Amish family?"

She shook her head. "I never imagined anything like this. Do you do it every year?"

"We do."

"You aren't going to actually sing, are you, John?"

He threw back his head and laughed. "*Nee*, but I will hum along."

"Softly, dear, softly," she suggested.

He wondered if she realized that she had called him *dear*. It was turning out to be an even more wonderful night than he had hoped for.

After thirty-five years as a nurse, **Patricia Davids** hung up her stethoscope to become a full-time writer. She enjoys spending her free time visiting her grandchildren, doing some long-overdue yard work and traveling to research her story locations. She resides in Wichita, Kansas. Pat always enjoys hearing from her readers. You can visit her online at patriciadavids.com.

Books by Patricia Davids

Love Inspired

The Amish Bachelors

An Amish Harvest
An Amish Noel
His Amish Teacher
Their Pretend Amish Courtship
Amish Christmas Twins

Lancaster Courtships

The Amish Midwife

Brides of Amish Country

Plain Admirer
Amish Christmas Joy
The Shepherd's Bride
The Amish Nanny
An Amish Family Christmas: A Plain Holiday
An Amish Christmas Journey
Amish Redemption

Visit the Author Profile page at Harlequin.com for more titles.

Millie Mahoney

Amish Christmas Twins

Patricia Davids

⟨H⟩ HARLEQUIN® LOVE INSPIRED®

LOVE INSPIRED BOOKS

Recycling programs for this product may not exist in your area.

ISBN-13: 978-0-373-62302-0

Amish Christmas Twins

www.Harlequin.com

Printed in U.S.A.

And all thy children shall be taught of the Lord;
and great shall be the peace of thy children.
—*Isaiah* 54:13

This book is happily dedicated to Tony Hill, a wonderful, helpful son-in-law and a loving stepfather to my two precious grandchildren.

Thanks, Tony, for all you do. Love you to pieces. Oh, and don't forget to mow my lawn.

Mama Pat

Chapter One

John Miller squeezed his eyes shut and braced for the impact of the bus hurtling toward the back of his wagon.

God have mercy on my soul.

A powerful draft knocked his hat from his head as the bus flew around him, missing his wagon by inches. The reckless driver laid on the horn as he swerved back into the proper lane. John's frightened team of horses shied off the edge of the highway, jolting the wagon and nearly unseating him.

He quickly brought his animals under control and maneuvered his wagon back onto the roadway. It took longer to get his heart out of his throat. When his erratic pulse settled, he picked up his black Amish hat from where it had fallen onto the floorboards and dusted it against his thigh. *God must still have a use for me here on earth. I'm sorry, Katie May. One day I will be with you again.*

John shook his head when the bus pulled to a stop a few hundred yards down the highway. "Foolish *Englischer.* In a hurry to get nowhere fast."

He settled his hat on his head and glanced back at

his cargo. Thankfully, the restored antique sleigh carefully wrapped in a heavy tarp hadn't shifted. He could ill afford another delay in getting it to its new owner.

His entire trip had been one misadventure after another. He'd left home in plenty of time to complete the two-day journey, but a wrong turn in unfamiliar country had taken him five miles out of his way. One of his tie-downs had snapped, forcing him to lose time rigging another. Then a broken wheel had taken three hours to repair, time he didn't have to spare. This simple trip could end up costing him as much if not more than a hired hauler would have charged and he was already half a day late for his appointment. He hoped his *Englisch* client was the understanding sort.

Putting his team in motion, John reached the rear of the bus before it moved on. According to the directions in the letter from his customer, he needed to turn right at the rural intersection just ahead. He waited for the bus driver to move out of the way. After several minutes, he leaned to the side trying to see what the holdup was. A woman in a red coat with a purple backpack slung over her shoulder finally stepped off with two little children in tow. The bus pulled away, belching black fumes that made his horses snort and toss their heads. He spoke softly to quiet them.

The woman stood at the edge of the highway, looking first north and then south as if expecting someone who hadn't shown up. The roads were empty in all directions except for the bus traveling away from them. The children, both girls about three years old, were clinging to her legs. One rubbed her eyes, the other cried to be picked up. The family's clothing and uncovered heads told John they weren't Amish.

He slapped the reins against his team's rumps and turned his wagon in front of them, glancing at the woman's face as he did. She looked worried and worn-out, but she smiled and nodded slightly when she met his gaze.

One of her little girls pointed to his team. "Horsey, Mama. See horsey?"

"I do, sweetheart. They're lovely horses, aren't they?" Her smile brightened as she glanced down at her daughter. The love in her eyes shone through her weariness. Why wasn't anyone here to meet them?

"Horses bad," the other child said, stepping behind her mother.

The woman dropped to one knee and pulled the child close. "No, they aren't bad. They may look big and scary, but they won't hurt you. This man tells them what to do. I'm sure they mind him far better than you mind me sometimes."

The child muttered something he couldn't make out, but the young mother laughed softly. It was a sweet sound. "No, precious. They won't step on you and squish you."

The child latched on to her mother's neck and muttered, "I tired. Want to go home now."

He should keep moving. He'd told his client to expect him four hours ago, but it didn't feel right to drive away and leave this young mother standing alone out here even if she wasn't Amish. He pulled the horses to a stop and looked down at her. "Do you need help?"

Detaching the child from her neck, she stood up and smoothed the front of her coat with one hand. As she did, he noticed a bulge at her waist. Was she pregnant?

"I'm trying to get my bearings. I haven't been out

this way in years. Do you know an Amish farmer named Ezekiel Lapp?"

Her voice was soft and low. He heard the weariness underlying her tone. The wind blew a strand of her shoulder-length blond curls across her face. She brushed her hair back and tucked it behind her ear as she looked at him with wide blue eyes.

She was a pretty woman. Her daughters, identical twins by the look of them, were the spitting images of her with blue eyes and curly blond hair. Some man was fortunate to have such handsome children and a lovely wife to come home to at night.

She placed a hand on each little girl's head in a comforting or perhaps protective gesture, her fingers moving gently through their hair. She raised her chin as she faced him.

The gesture reminded him of his wife, Katie, and sent a painful pang through his chest. Katie used to give him that exact look when she was determined to do things her own way. The woman at the roadside wasn't physically similar to his wife. She was tiny where Katie had been tall and willowy. She was fair where Katie had been dark, but the two women shared the same stubborn set to their chins and the same determination in their eyes. He smiled in spite of himself.

Katie would have been a good mother, too…if only she had lived.

He shut away his heartbreaking memories. Katie May was gone, their unborn child laid to rest with her. It had been four years since their passing, but his grief was as sharp as if it had been yesterday. Most folks thought he had moved on with his life. He'd tried to, but he couldn't forgive God or himself for her death.

He looked away from the young woman and her children. "I don't know him. I'm not from this area."

Realizing how gruff his voice sounded, he gestured to the tarp on the flatbed wagon behind him. It had taken him eight weeks to restore the sleigh and two days to haul it this far. He was anxious to drop it off and head home. "I'm delivering this sleigh to Melvin Taylor. The directions he sent said he lived four miles south of this intersection. Does that help?"

Her face brightened. "I remember Melvin. He lived a half mile south of Grandfather's farm. We can find our way now. Thank you. Come on, girls." She repositioned the backpack on her shoulder and took each girl by the hand as she started down the road.

John didn't urge his horses to move. A three-and-a-half-mile walk was a lot to ask of such small children, and the woman if she was pregnant. It would be dark before they arrived at their destination. The mid-November day had been pleasant so far, but it would get cold when the sun started to go down.

He didn't normally concern himself with the affairs of the *Englisch*, but something about this young woman kept him from driving away. Maybe it was the worry he had glimpsed on her face when he first saw her, or how she spoke so caringly to her girls. Perhaps it was the way she squared her shoulders, looking as if she carried a great weight upon them. He didn't know what it was, but he couldn't leave without offering her assistance.

Maybe it was because she reminded him of Katie.

This is foolish. They'll be fine on their own. An Amish family wouldn't think twice about walking that far.

However, an Amish mother and her children would be properly dressed with heavy coats and sturdy shoes.

The thin white shoes on this woman's feet didn't look as if they would last a mile. He sighed heavily and urged his team forward to catch up with her.

He pulled his horses to a halt beside her. "It's a long walk, *frau*. I can give you a lift. I'm going in the same direction."

She stopped walking and eyed him with obvious indecision. "That's very kind of you, but I don't want to put you to any trouble."

"It's no trouble." It was, but it would trouble him more to leave her.

"We'll be fine." She started walking again.

Stubborn woman. "It will be dark before you get there. The *kinder*, the children, already look tired."

She glanced at her girls and then at him. "You're right, they are tired. It was a long bus ride from…home." Her gaze slid away from his.

He didn't care where she was from or why she didn't want to share that information. The more time he spent reasoning with her, the longer his client would be waiting. He leaned toward her. "Then hand the children up to me and save them a long walk."

She hesitated, chewing on the corner of her lower lip.

Exasperated, he was ready to leave her and get on with his journey. "You'll be safe with me, *frau*, if that is what worries you."

"That's exactly what a serial killer would say."

He scowled at her but noticed the twinkle in her eyes as she tried to hide a smile. "Are you teasing me?"

She grinned. "I was trying to, but I fear I have offended you."

The *Englisch* were a strange lot. "I take no offense. Give over your *kinder*."

He took each child she lifted to him and settled them on the bench seat, knowing he would likely be sorry for his generosity before long. The children would whine and cry, and the woman would probably talk his ear off. He offered her his hand.

A blush stained her cheeks rosy pink. "I'm not as light as the girls."

He almost laughed at the absurd notion that she was too heavy to lift. "I can get you up here without undue effort…unless your pockets are full of bricks. Are they?"

A smile twitched at the corner of her lips. "They aren't, but you may think so."

Her sweet expression pulled a chuckle from him in return. "I doubt that."

She slipped her hand in his. Her fingers were soft and dainty compared to his big calloused paw. He'd almost forgotten what it was like to hold a woman's hand, how it made a man feel strong and protective. Gazing into her upturned face, he was drawn to the humor lingering in her blue eyes. Sunlight glinted on her hair as the breeze tugged at her curls. He easily pulled her up to the wagon seat. The delicate scent of jasmine reached him. Was it her perfume?

Amish women never wore perfume. It was considered worldly to do so and was thus forbidden, but the fragrance of this young woman reminded John of summer evenings spent on his grandmother's porch as the bees hummed around the hanging plants she had cherished. Perhaps he would buy a plant in the spring to remind him of his grandmother and of this young mother.

He slowly released her hand and forced himself to concentrate on his horses. "Walk on, Jake. Get along, Pete."

* * *

Willa Chase glanced from under her lashes at the man beside her. Her Amish Good Samaritan had amazing strength. He had lifted her pregnant bulk with one hand as easily as he had lifted her three-year-old daughters. Seated beside him, she felt dwarfed by his size, but, oddly, he didn't intimidate her. He had spoken gruffly at first, but there was a gentle kindness beneath his teasing that put her at ease.

It was an unusual feeling for her. Before her husband died, he had taught her not to be the trusting sort. Perhaps she'd made an exception because this man was Amish. She had been Amish once, too. A very long time ago. To keep her children safe, she would become Amish again. Then Willa Chase and her daughters would disappear forever.

"I like horsey. Like horsey man," Lucy said, giving their driver a shy smile.

"Horse bad. Man bad." Megan glared at him and stuck out her lower lip as if daring him to argue with her.

"No, he isn't bad, Megan." Willa slanted a glance at the man beside her. As was typical of married Amish men, he wore a beard but no mustache. "I'm sorry about that, sir."

He shrugged. "Little ones speak the truth as they see it."

Relieved that he wasn't offended, she smiled her thanks. "You must have children of your own if you know how embarrassing they can be."

His expression hardened. "*Nee, Gott* has not blessed me with *kinder.*"

His tone said the conversation was over. Remembering how much her Amish grandfather had disliked idle chitchat, Willa whispered to her girls, "We must be quiet so we don't scare the horses or annoy our new friend."

She settled them against her sides, hoping they would fall asleep again as they had on the bus. Willa remained silent, too. The less she said, the better. She couldn't believe she had let slip that she was going to her grandfather's farm, but at least she'd caught herself before she blurted out where they were from.

God had been looking out for her when He sent this man to aid her. Unlike some of the talkative, nosy people on the bus who were full of questions about the twins, an Amish person was unlikely to be inquisitive. Most believed it was impolite to question strangers. Others worried they might be speaking to a shunned former member and would choose silence out of caution. Either way, it worked to her advantage now.

Soon they would be safe with her grandfather. She refused to think about what would happen if he turned them away. He wouldn't. She had to believe that.

The rocking of the wagon, the jingle of the harnesses and the steady clip-clop of the horses' hooves slowly soothed the tenseness from her muscles. She closed her eyes to rest them just for a minute.

The moment she opened the door and saw a police officer standing in the hall outside their apartment in a run-down section of Columbus, Willa knew something terrible had happened. An accident, the officer said. A hit-and-run. Glen was dead. They were still looking for the driver. At least the police officer didn't take her daughters away from her.

Willa stumbled through the following days of grief with leaden feet. After writing to inform Glen's parents, she moved again. Glen had always been the one to say when and where they went. He knew how to erase their trail—only no matter how often they moved, he would inevitably come home one day and say they had to go again. His parents were closing in. She shared Glen's deep-seated fear without knowing why. She knew only that his parents had the power and the money to take the children away. They said she was an unfit mother. She had been, but she was better now. Glen was the one who knew what to do. How could she fight his parents without him? She was pregnant, broke and on her own against their terrible scheme. She could think of only one way to keep her children safe. She had to run.

Someone grabbed her arm. Willa jerked upright. It took her a few seconds to gather her foggy wits. The wagon had stopped moving. She found her Amish Good Samaritan staring at her.

"You were asleep. I feared you'd *falla* out *da* wagon."

She checked her daughters and found them awake, too. "I guess I was more tired than I thought."

He released her. "Is this your grandfather's place?"

She looked past him and saw a mailbox for E. Lapp. A glance up the lane proved she had arrived at her destination, for she recognized the farm where she'd grown up. "It is. Girls, we are here. Thank the nice man for giving us a ride."

Lucy did. Megan only glared at him. Willa got down and lifted them off the wagon without his help. He touched the brim of his hat and drove on. He glanced back once. Willa knew because she was still standing by the mailbox looking after him. She raised her hand in a simple wave. He did the same and then turned back to the road.

The Amish were quiet, kind, peaceful people. Willa had forgotten how unassuming they could be during the years she had been away. Her Good Samaritan hadn't asked a single question about who she was or why she was in the middle of nowhere with two little children. She was glad he hadn't. She hated the idea that she might have had to lie to him.

She watched the burly man drive away with a sense of loss, almost as if she were losing a gentle giant of a friend. Although he was a stranger, she had felt safe in his company. For the first time since her panicked flight from Columbus, she felt hopeful about her decision to return to her Amish grandfather. It had to be the right choice. She didn't have another option.

She cupped a hand over her abdomen and raised her chin. Time was short, but she would find a safe place for her daughters and her unborn baby before it was too late.

Adjusting her bag on her shoulder, she shepherded her tired girls up the dirt lane. When she drew close to the house, she saw an elderly man standing on the farmhouse steps. It had been ten years since they'd last met. It wasn't a time she liked to recall. She stopped a few feet away. "Hello, Grandfather."

Ezekiel Lapp's weathered face gave no indication of what he was thinking. His dark Amish clothing, full gray beard and black hat added to his somber appearance, but he was frailer and thinner than she remembered. Her daughters clung to her legs as they peered at him from behind her.

"Why have you come?" he asked.

"I wanted you to meet my daughters. This is Megan and this is Lucy." Willa placed a hand behind their heads and urged them to step forward. Lucy faced him, but Megan spun around and retreated behind Willa again.

"Hi." Lucy opened and closed her fingers to wave at him.

"Where is your *Englisch* husband?" Ezekiel asked, ignoring the child.

"Glen passed away six months ago."

"It was *Gott*'s will, but I am sorry for your loss," Ezekiel said softly in Pennsylvania Deitsh, the language of the Amish.

Willa blinked back tears. The pain was still fresh in her heart. "*Danki.* Thank you."

"Mama is sad," Megan said.

"I sad," Lucy added. "I'm cold, Mama."

The early fall wind had a bite to it. Willa shivered despite the coat she wore. It wasn't heavy enough, but it was the only one she had that she could button across her pregnant stomach.

"Come inside." Ezekiel turned and went in the house without waiting for them.

Relief made Willa's knees weak. *So far, so good.*

She had no idea what she would do if he turned them away. She had spent the last of her money to get this far. Unless her grandfather took them in, they would be sleeping in a barn or under a bridge tonight. She climbed the steps with the girls close beside her.

Inside the house, little had changed since the day her parents walked away from their Amish life with her in tow. The wide plank floor of the kitchen had been scrubbed clean. A simple table with four chairs sat in the center of the room. The windows were free of shades or curtains, for an upright Amish family in her grandfather's ultraconservative church had nothing to hide from the outside world. A single plate, cup and fork in the dish drainer by the sink proved her grandfather still lived alone. The room smelled faintly of bleach and stout coffee. The scent transported her to the past the way nothing else had done.

She had been fifteen the last time she stood in this room, completely confused by the family quarrel taking place. One day she was Amish and knew her place in the world. She knew what was expected of her. She had been a week away from her baptism. The next week she was an awkward, shy, frightened girl trying to fit into the perplexing English world her parents had chosen.

Her Amish childhood had been filled with hard work, but she had been happy here. If her grandfather took them in, she could be happy here again. Nothing mattered as long as she had her children with her.

She led her girls to the heavy wood-burning cookstove and held out her hands to the welcome heat. "Don't touch. It's very hot," she cautioned them.

"Are your children hungry?" her grandfather asked, speaking *Deitsh.*

"I'm sure they are."

"Have them sit." He walked to the counter and opened a drawer.

Willa helped the girls out of their coats and seated them at the table. She hung their coats on pegs by the front door and then stood behind her daughters, not daring to assume the invitation included her.

He scowled when he turned around. "Sit. I will not

eat with you, but I am permitted to feed the hungry as our Lord commanded us. Then you must go."

Willa's heart sank, but she held on to the hope that he would change his mind when he learned the details of her situation. She took a seat at the table and waited while her grandfather prepared church spread for her daughters.

A mixture of peanut butter, marshmallow cream and maple syrup, the tasty treat was often served on bread or used as a dip for apples or pears. He spread it on thick slices of homemade bread and set it on plates in front of them. It was just as good as Willa remembered...

The girls loved it. When they were finished eating, she led them to the stark living room and settled them for a nap on the sofa.

When she was sure they were sleeping, she returned to the kitchen. Her grandfather sat at the table with a cup of coffee in his hands.

She stood across from him and laid a protective hand on her stomach. "I have no money. I have no job. I don't have a place to live, and my baby is due the second week of January."

Willa thought she glimpsed a flash of sympathy in his eyes. "Your husband's family will not help you?"

A chill slipped over her skin. She crossed her arms to ward it off. They were the ones claiming she was an unfit mother because of her mental breakdown. According to Glen, they had paid an unscrupulous judge to grant them custody of the twins while she was in the hospital. Willa knew nothing about the law, but without money and without Glen to help her, they would succeed in taking her children away. She couldn't allow that. "*Nee*, you are my last hope."

* * *

Her grandfather took a sip of his coffee. "I have no money to give you."

"I don't want money. I wish to return to the Amish faith." She held her breath, hoping he believed her.

He was silent for a long time. She waited and prayed for his forgiveness and for his understanding.

He shook his head. "I can't help you. You must go."

She couldn't bear to hear those words. Not after she had come so far. Tears sprang to her eyes, but she blinked them back. "Please, I'm begging you. I have nowhere else to go. Don't turn us away. We are your flesh and blood."

His brow darkened. "You come to me wearing *Englisch* clothes, with your shorn hair and your head uncovered. I see no repentance in you. I have heard none from your lips, yet you say you want to be Amish again. You share in the shame your father brought to this house."

"I was a child. I had no choice but to go with my parents."

"You chose to remain in the *Englisch* world all these years, even after the death of my son and his wife. You could have come back then. I would have taken you in. *Nee*, I will not help you now. This suffering, you have brought on yourself." He rose, put on his hat and coat and went out the door.

Willa sat at the table and dropped her head on her crossed arms as she gave in to despair. Gut-wrenching sobs shook her body. Why was God doing this? Hadn't she suffered enough? How much more would He ask of her?

Chapter Two

"I'm sorry I'm late. I had a few unexpected delays." John stepped down from his wagon as Melvin Taylor came out of the house to meet him.

"You said you'd be here today. It's still today." Melvin pushed the brim of his red ball cap up with one finger and grinned.

Relief made John smile. Melvin appeared to be the understanding sort and a rare *Englisch* fellow in John's book—one who wasn't in a rush. His hopes for more work from the man rose.

"Can't thank you enough for taking on my little project."

"I enjoyed restoring it." He loved re-creating useful things from the past.

Melvin rubbed his hands together. "Well, don't keep me in suspense any longer. How did it turn out?"

"I'll let you be the judge." Moving to the back of the wagon, John untied the ropes and lifted the tarp covering his load. The antique blue-and-gold sleigh had made the journey unharmed.

"I knew she was a beauty under all that neglect."

Melvin drew his fingers along the smooth, elaborately curved metal runner. "I'm right pleased with your work, John Miller."

"Danki."

It had taken John weeks to duplicate all the missing pieces in his forge and assemble it. After he replaced the tattered upholstery with a plush blue tufted fabric, the result was well worth his time and effort. The Portland Cutter would glide through the snow as neatly now as it had a hundred and fifty years ago.

He had managed to turn back the hands of time for the sleigh. If only he could change one hour of the past for himself.

Such a thing wasn't possible. He had to spend the rest of his life knowing his pride had cost the life of the only woman he would ever love. His penance was to go on living without her. Hard work at his forge was the only way he kept the long hours of loneliness at bay.

Melvin stepped back from the wagon with a big grin on his face. "Would you be willing to take on another project for me?"

John tried not to sound too eager. "I'd have to see it first and we would have to agree on a price."

"Sure. I think you'll like my latest find."

John followed the childishly eager man to a large shed. Melvin pushed open the sliding door with a flourish to reveal a half dozen sleighs. Five were in pristine condition. Only one needed restoration work. A lot of work.

Melvin patted the faded front seat, sending a small cloud of dust into the air. "I found this vis-à-vis sleigh at a farm sale about an hour north of here."

John walked around the vehicle, assessing what

needed to be fixed. Vis-à-vis sleighs were easily recognizable. They consisted of a raised coachman's seat and two lower passenger seats behind the driver that faced each other. They had originally been used in cities where well-to-do people were driven about during the winter to parties and such.

He checked the floorboards first. They were rotten. That was to be expected. Three of the ornate lantern holders were missing, but he could duplicate them from the one remaining. The runners looked sound. They must have been repaired at some time in the past. The upholstery definitely needed replacing, but the wooden frames of the seats looked in good shape. "I can have it ready in three weeks, maybe less."

He could finish it in two weeks, but he didn't want to lock himself into a shorter time frame. More pressing work might come up. Better to finish earlier than promised rather than later.

"Awesome. To have it finished before Christmas, that will be great. Let's hope for plenty of snow." They agreed on the price and the men shook hands.

"Shall I ship it to you?" Melvin asked as they walked toward the door.

"I figured the cost of transporting it home and bringing it back myself in my estimate. If I have to hire someone to ship it back, that will be an additional charge."

"Agreed. I'll help you get the other one unloaded and this one strapped on, and then we can have a cup of coffee. The missus put on a fresh pot when she saw you drive in." The two men walked toward the house.

Unbidden, the thought of the young mother he'd met earlier entered John's mind. He should have asked her name. Melvin might know. Although her business was

cause to worry about a stranger and her family. He would never see them again. They were in God's hands.

Willa raised her head and saw it was almost dark outside. She must have fallen asleep. Her head hurt from crying. She rose stiffly and stretched her aching back, then wiped her damp cheeks as she looked around. Were the girls still sleeping? That would be unusual.

She checked in the living room. The sofa was empty. She called their names, but neither of them answered. Where were they? Panic uncoiled inside her. Their coats were gone from the pegs where she had hung them. She yanked open the front door and saw them come out of the barn walking beside her grandfather.

Lucy saw her first and came running. "Mama, I saw a cow."

Willa's pounding heart slowed with relief. She dropped to one knee and hugged Lucy. "Did you? Was she a nice cow?"

Lucy nodded. "She licked her nose like this." Lucy stuck her tongue out and tried to touch it to her nose.

"Cows poo in the dirt," Megan said with a look of disgust.

Willa held back a chuckle as she rose to her feet. She stepped aside as her grandfather carried a red pail of fresh milk up the steps. From under the porch, half a dozen kittens came out meowing for their supper. Her grandfather handed Megan the pail. "Pour this in the pan for the kittens."

"I help." Lucy grabbed the side of the pail. The two girls poured out the milk while the kittens tumbled around their feet and into the aluminum pie pan.

She left Megan and Lucy to play with the cats and followed her grandfather inside.

"Thank you for watching the girls and letting me sleep."

"You were worn-out."

"I was. It has been a long time since I've had a peaceful night's rest."

He was silent for a long moment, then he glanced toward the porch. The girls were still playing with the kittens. "Out in the barn Megan told me that bad people are looking for her and Lucy. What did she mean?"

Willa decided to tell him and took a seat at the table. After all, what did she have to lose? "My husband, Glen, had a falling-out with his parents before he met me. He would never talk about it except to say that they wanted to lock him up. He was a good man. I can't believe he did anything wrong."

Even as she defended him, she knew it wasn't entirely true. Glen found it easy to assume new identities and fabricate stories about where they came from without remorse, but he had been good to her.

"Go on," her grandfather said.

"He was always worried that they would find us. We moved three times the first year we were married. Then the girls were born."

Shame burned in Willa's throat, but she forced herself to continue. "Trying to take care of fussy twins wore us down. I'm not making excuses, but it was hard. We didn't have any help. Glen had to work and I was home alone with the babies. I never got enough sleep. I became...sick."

Her grandfather wouldn't understand the terrible things she had done. How could he when she didn't understand them herself. She should have been stronger. The doctors at the hospital had called it postpartum psychosis. The voices telling her to hide her babies from Glen hadn't been real. They had been delusions, but she had done all they told her to do, even wading into the cold, rain-swollen river with the babies in her arms. They all would have died that night if not for the quick-thinking intervention of a stranger.

Willa realized she had been staring into the past, trying to remember all that had happened, but so much of her memory was blank. "I spent four weeks in a hospital. Glen couldn't manage alone. He contacted his parents, believing they would help for the sake of their grandchildren. They came, but they only wanted to take the girls away from us. They said we were unfit parents and that the law was on their side."

Tears slipped down Willa's cheeks and she brushed them away. Tears wouldn't help anything. She had to be strong. It was up to her now. "Glen managed to get away with the babies before the police came. He picked me up at the hospital and we left town with only the clothes on our backs. We tried to start over, but we had to move so many times I lost count. After Glen died, I didn't know what to do except to come here. If his parents find me, they will take the girls away and I'll never see them again."

"Will the *Englisch* police come here?"

"Maybe, I can't be sure. I was careful not to tell anyone where I was going. I purchased a ticket for the next town down the road, but I got off the bus before then. People on the bus may remember us. An Amish fellow gave us a lift here, but he wasn't from this area. I do know Glen's parents won't stop looking for the girls, but it will be hard to find us among the Amish."

He stared into his coffee cup for a long time. Finally, he glanced at her. "Up in the attic you will find a black trunk. There are clothes that you and the girls can wear in it. They will be warmer than what they have on now. They are *goot* Amish clothes. If you mean to rejoin the faith, you must dress plain."

"Does this mean we can stay?" She was afraid to hope.

"With me, *nee*. Go to my sister, Ada Kaufman. She was also shunned by our church, but I hear she has kept to the Amish ways in a new church group in Hope Springs."

Willa had fond memories of her great-aunt Ada, a kindly and spry woman with a son and daughter a few years older than Willa. A flicker of hope came alive inside her chest. She still had family she could go to.

The thought of spending Christmas with her aunt and cousins Miriam and Mark made Willa smile. They'd had some fine times together in the old days. Her cousins might be married with children of their own by now. Her daughters could have cousins to celebrate the holidays with the way she once did.

"Do you think Ada will help me?"

"That, I cannot say. I have an old buggy and a horse you can use to travel there."

"How far is it?" Willa had never heard of Hope Springs.

"Three days' travel to the east, more or less."

Three days by buggy with the girls. It would be next to impossible. Where would they stay at night? What would they eat? She had no money. And yet, what choice did she have except to go on faith? There was no going back now. "*Danki, Daddi.* What made you change your mind?"

"Your children deserve the chance to know our ways. I pray *Gott* opens your heart and that you seek true repentance. When you do so, you will be welcomed here."

"I'll send you money for the horse and buggy when I can," she promised.

"I want no money from you. They are a gift to your children. You may all sleep upstairs in your old room, but you must leave at first light on Monday."

It wasn't what she had hoped for, but she wasn't beaten yet. Perhaps her great-aunt's family would be like the kind Amish man she had met that afternoon. The memory of his solid presence and quiet kindness filled her heart with renewed hope. She wished she had been bold enough to ask his name. She would remember him in her prayers.

Three days after delivering his restored sleigh, John was home and hard at work on his new project. The coals in his forge glowed red-hot with each injection of air from his bellows. Sweat poured down his face. He tasted salt and ashes on his lips, but he didn't move back. The fire was almost hot enough. Using long tongs, he held a flat piece of iron bar stock in the glowing coals, waiting until it reached the right temperature to be shaped by his hammer. A black heat would be too cold. A white heat would be too hot. A good working heat was the red-orange glow he was waiting on. The smell of smoke and hot metal filled the cold air around him.

Movement out on the road that fronted his property caught his attention. He let go of the tongs and shaded his eyes with one hand to see against the glare of the late-afternoon sun. Was his mother coming home from the quilting bee already? He didn't expect her for another hour.

A buggy approached the top of the hill, but it wasn't one he knew. He didn't recognize the skinny horse between the shafts, either. He'd put shoes on nearly every horse in the area. He knew them and their owners on sight. This was someone new, and he or she was driving erratically.

The horse trotted up the road veering from side to side in a tired, rambling gait. Its black hide was flecked with white foam, but it kept going. The road led uphill to where his lane turned off at the crest. Just beyond that, the road sloped downward for a few hundred yards before it ended in a T where it intersected the blacktop highway that skirted the edge of the river just beyond. The tired horse crested the hill and stumbled but didn't turn in John's lane. As it went past, John realized there wasn't anyone in the driver's seat.

It was a runaway. Without someone to stop it, the horse was likely to trot straight across the highway into traffic and perhaps even into the river.

John let go of the bellows, sprinted up his lane and out into the road after the buggy. Had the horse been fresh, he wouldn't stand a chance of catching it, but it was tiring. The steep climb had slowed it.

"Whoa there, whoa," he shouted, praying the horse was well trained and would respond to the command. It kept going. Sprinting harder, he raced after the vehicle, his lungs burning like his forge. There was traffic below on the highway. A horse-drawn wagon loaded with hay slowed several cars, but one after the other, they pulled out and sped around him. The buggy was unlikely to make it across without being hit.

Running up behind the vehicle, John realized it was a Swartzentruber buggy. The most conservative group among the Amish, the Swartzentruber didn't fit their buggies with the slow-moving-vehicle sign, windshields, mirrors or electric lighting. One rear wheel wobbled heavily. He finally drew close enough to grab the rear door handle. Yanking it open, he gave one final burst of effort and threw himself inside, no easy task for a man of his size.

The buggy wasn't empty. There were two little girls in black bonnets holding on to each other in the back seat. They started screaming when they saw him.

"Shush, shush. *Ich bin freind*." He spoke in *Deitsh*, telling them he was a friend. He quickly climbed over the seatback. An Amish woman lay slumped on the floorboards, her face obscured by the large black traveling bonnet she wore. The reins had fallen out of her hands but not out of the buggy. He glanced out the front and saw the horse was nearly at the bottom of the hill. The highway was less than ten yards away.

John grabbed the reins and pulled back as he stomped on the buggy brake. The foam-flecked black mare stumbled to a halt and hung her head, her sides heaving as a car zipped past. The poor horse didn't even flinch.

John quickly checked the woman on the floor. She was dressed in a heavy black winter coat, gloves and a black traveling bonnet. He could see she was breathing. He tried rousing her without success by shaking her shoulder. He had no idea what was wrong. The girls in back kept crying for their mama.

After lifting the woman onto the seat, he spoke to the

girls again in *Deitsh*. "What are your names? Do you live near here? What is your papa's name?"

They were too frightened or too shy to answer him. As he pulled his arm from behind the woman's head, he noticed a smear of blood on his sleeve. He untied her bonnet and removed it. Her *kapp* came off with it and her blond curls sprang free. His breath caught in his throat as he recognized the woman he'd given a lift to several days before.

What was Willa Lapp doing here?

The side of her head was matted with dried blood, but the wound under it was only a shallow gash. Had she struck her head hard enough to be knocked unconscious, or had she hurt herself when she fell? He had no way of knowing.

He asked the children what had happened, but they only stared at him fearfully without answering. He would have to wait until the woman could answer all his questions when she came to.

Leaving her settled more comfortably on the seat, he stepped forward to check on the horse and noticed a piece of harness hanging loose. It had been repaired with a loop of wire at some time in the past. The wire had snapped, leaving a sharp point sticking through the leather. The flapping piece of harness had been jabbing the mare's side with each step she took, forcing her to keep moving even as she was close to exhaustion.

Now what? John pulled on the tip of his beard as he looked around. He couldn't ask the trembling, exhausted horse to pull the buggy back up the steep hill. He didn't want to leave two crying children and an unconscious woman at the side of the road until he could return with a fresh horse. The mare had to be walked until she cooled down or she would sicken in this cold. It left him with only one option. He had to take them all together.

The girls had stopped crying and were huddled behind their mother. She hadn't stirred. He found a horse blanket beneath the back seat, unhitched the mare and covered her with it. Leading her back to the buggy door, he opened it and held out his hand to the nearest child. "*Kumm*, we *lawfa*."

She pushed his hand aside. "Bad man. Go away."

The other girl patted her mother's face. "Is Mama sick?"

He switched to English. "*Ja*, your mother is sick. I will take you to my house. Come, we must walk there."

They looked at each other with uncertainty. He slipped his arms beneath their mother and lifted her out of the buggy. His suspicion that Willa was pregnant proved to be true. Starting up the hill with his burden, he glanced back. The children climbed down and hurried after him, giving a wide berth to the horse he was leading. They reached his side and stayed close, holding hands with each other as they struggled to keep up with his long strides. He slowed his pace.

One of the girls caught hold of his coat. "Horsey man, wait."

He stopped walking. "I'm not horsey man. My name is John, John Miller."

"Johnjohn." She grinned at him.

"Just John, and what is your name?"

"Lucy. Is Mama okay?"

"You are all okay thanks to God's mercy this day." He had stopped this woman's buggy from running into traffic and being hit by a car. Why hadn't someone stopped Katie May's buggy before it had been smashed to bits and her life snuffed out?

Why hadn't he stopped his wife from leaving that day? It was a question that haunted his days and nights.

The woman in his arms moaned, pulling his mind from the past. He started walking again. She wasn't heavy, but his arms were burning by the time he reached the front steps of his house. He dropped the horse's reins and hoped she was too tired to wander off until he got his unexpected guests settled. This was costing him valuable time away from his forge and wasting fuel. He didn't like interruptions when he was working.

He carried her into the living room, laid her on the sofa and then knelt beside her. The little girls pressed close to him.

"Mama's sleeping," whispered the one who'd told him her name was Lucy. The only way he could tell them apart was that Lucy still had her bonnet on. The other sister had taken hers off somewhere between the buggy and his front step.

He gazed down at Willa's peaceful face. Her dark blond eyelashes were fanned against fair cheeks framed by golden curls. She was even prettier than he remembered.

He shook off his unusually fanciful thoughts and gave her injury closer inspection. The gash wasn't deep, but the fact that she hadn't roused had him worried. He unbuttoned her coat to check for other injures and found none. He pulled his hands away. He had no idea what to do with an unconscious pregnant woman.

Lucy tugged on his coat sleeve. "I'm hungry."

The other child crossed her legs. "I need to go potty."

He sat back on his heels in consternation. Where was his mother when he needed her?

Chapter Three

$\smallsmile$

Willa heard voices she didn't recognize. Were they real, or was she hallucinating? The psychosis wouldn't start before her baby was born, would it? Her hands went to her stomach. Reassured by the feel of her unborn child nestled there, she opened her eyes. She was in a room she'd never seen before. Where were her girls? She tried to sit up. Pain lanced through her head, sending a burst of nausea to her empty stomach. She closed her eyes, hoping it would recede. She needed to find her children.

"Take it easy," a man's voice said close beside her.

She turned her head to see someone looming above her. She blinked hard, and he swam into focus. He was a mountain of a man with broad shoulders and a black beard that covered his jawline and chin. He knelt beside her and slipped an arm under her shoulders to ease her upright. His dark brown hair was cut in a bowl style she remembered from her youth. He was Amish or perhaps Old Order Mennonite. The beard meant he was a married man. His eyes were a rich coffee brown with crow's feet at the corners. She thought she read sympathy in their depths. The longer she looked at him, the more convinced she was that they had met before, but her mind was so fuzzy she couldn't remember where.

She clutched his arm as she struggled to get up. "Where are my daughters?"

His muscles were rock hard beneath her fingers. The feel of his steely arms was reassuring. It triggered her memory. She did know him. This was the man who had kindly given her a ride to her grandfather's farm.

"Relax. Your children are with my *mudder*. She is getting them something to eat." He patted her hand, and she let go of him. He sat back on a chair at the end of the sofa.

Willa had to see them for herself. "Lucy, Megan, come here!" A deep, harsh cough sent burning pain through her chest. Her cold was getting worse.

The pair hurried through the open doorway. "Mama, you awake?" Megan asked.

Her little worrier. Older than her sister by five minutes and a hundred years. Willa pulled both girls to her in a fierce hug. "Yes, I'm awake."

Megan scowled and took Willa's face between her hands. "Don't fall down!"

"I'm sorry I frightened you." She kissed Megan's hair and noticed her Amish *kapp* was missing. Willa had had trouble keeping the unfamiliar head covering on the girls. They didn't like them.

"I got peanut butter and jelly." Lucy offered her half-eaten sandwich to her mother. "Want some?"

Willa shook her head, ignoring the pain the movement caused. "I'm fine. You finish it."

"Okeydokey." Lucy didn't need further urging. She bit into her food with relish and was soon licking her fingers. The girls hadn't eaten since yesterday morning when they'd finished the last of the bread her grandfather had grudgingly given them. Willa hadn't had anything for two days, not since leaving her grandfather's farm. Her stomach growled loudly.

An elderly woman in Amish garb came to the doorway. "*Kinder, kumma* to the *dish* and let your *mamm* rest."

Megan leaned in to whisper in Willa's ear. "She talks funny."

The man seated beside Willa cleared his throat. She had almost forgotten that he was there. "My *mudder* doesn't speak *Englisch* often, so it is *goot* for her to practice."

Lucy hurried after the woman. "I want another sandwich, please."

Megan followed her. "Me, too."

Lucy frowned at her sister. "My sandwich, not yours!"

"I want one!" Megan fisted her hands on her hips.

"Lucy, Megan, you can each have your own sandwich," Willa said to end the mutiny she saw brewing. Their normal bickering relieved her mind. They didn't seem traumatized by what had happened.

Now that she knew her girls were safe, she turned her attention to the man at the end of the sofa. "How did we get here, and where is here?"

He scowled at her. "I have many questions for you, too. I happened to notice your buggy going past my lane with no one driving. I assumed it was a runaway and ran to catch it. Your girls were in the back seat and you were unconscious on the floorboard up front. What happened to you?"

She raised a hand to her aching head. She found a

bandage above her temple. "I must have fainted and hit my head. I haven't been feeling well." She didn't tell him she hadn't eaten. Another deep cough followed her words and left her head spinning.

"You don't remember what happened?"

They'd slept in the buggy again last night. Rather, the girls had slept. Willa's nagging cough had kept her awake. She had a vague memory of hitching up the horse at dawn. After that, only bits and pieces of traveling along the winding roadways came to mind. Nothing about how she had hurt her head.

"I don't remember much after starting out on the road this morning."

He eyed her intently. "You are not Amish and yet you and your children are dressed in our way and traveling by buggy. Why? What are you doing here? How did you find me?"

She scowled at his rapid-fire questions. "I wasn't looking for you."

"You told me you were visiting your grandfather, Ezekiel Lapp."

"I did see Grandfather. He gave me the horse and buggy so that I could visit other family members." Even with this kind man, she couldn't bring herself to share information about her destination. She'd spent too many years hiding where she was from and where she was going.

She knew the Amish bonnets would fool the casual observers, but not the real deal. Willa Chase and her children had to disappear. Someone looking for them wouldn't look twice at an Amish woman traveling with two children in a buggy. This man already knew she wasn't Amish, so she decided to tell him the truth, just not the whole truth.

"My parents left the church when I was young. I have decided to return to the faith and raise my children to be Amish, but I wanted to get reacquainted with my other relatives and spend Christmas with them before I decide where to settle."

"You are not shunned?"

She looked at him in surprise. "No. I wasn't baptized when my parents made the decision to leave. They were shunned by our congregation, but my parents are both gone now."

He studied her for a long moment, then nodded. "Our ways are *goot* ways to raise *kinder*. This is also the wish of your husband?"

Willa stared at her hands clenched together in her lap. "He died last May."

Her life had been a constant struggle since the horrible moment she received the news that Glen had been killed. Now that her grandfather had turned her away, she had one slim hope left—that her Amish great-aunt Ada or perhaps her cousin Mark or her cousin Miriam would take them in.

"I am sorry you lost your husband. I know it must have been difficult for you," the man said softly.

The compassion in his voice touched her deeply. *"Danki."*

She put aside her grief and focused on the present. "And thank you for stopping my runaway carriage. You have come to my rescue twice now and I don't even know your name."

"John Miller. My mother is Vera Miller."

"I'm Willa Lapp." She gave her maiden name, unable

to look John Miller in the eyes as she did so. "You have already met my daughters, Megan and Lucy. Where are we?"

His mother came in and handed Willa a steaming bowl of chicken soup and a spoon. "Eat. Your babe needs nourishment."

Willa took a sip and the hot, delicious broth drove away her nausea. "This is good. *Danki.*"

"Eat it all." The woman went back to the kitchen.

"You are at my home near Bowmans Crossing," John said.

The soup was warming Willa from the inside out. The chunks of chicken were tender and the noodles were the thick homemade kind her mother used to make. The name of the town he mentioned didn't ring a bell. "Is that close to Hope Springs?"

He shook his head. "You are a long way from there and traveling in the wrong direction if that is where you're headed."

She digested this unwelcome news. She had hoped to find her great-aunt before dark. She didn't want to spend another night on the open road. "Thank you for your help, but I must get going."

"Your horse needs rest and your buggy needs repairs. I can fix it, but it will take some time."

Disappointment weighed her down. She was so tired. Why couldn't one thing go right? "I'm afraid I can't pay you for any repairs."

"I have not asked for payment."

He rose and took the empty bowl from her hands. "You need rest, Willa Lapp. Don't worry about your *kinder. Mamm* will look after them. She also is not a killer of serials."

Willa had to smile at his mistaken turn of the phrase. "The term is *serial killer*."

She remembered how difficult it could be to translate the Pennsylvania Deitsh language of her youth into English. An Amish fellow might say he would go the road up and turn the gate in.

John frowned slightly as he repeated her words, "Serial killer. *Danki*. She is also not one of those. She has fixed a bed for you."

Willa wanted to protest, but she could barely keep her eyes open. She did need rest. Just a short nap while he fixed her buggy, then she would be on her way. She prayed her great-aunt would be as kind to her as this man and his mother had been.

Her eyes drifted closed. She barely noticed when John's mother came back into the room. "Bring her, John, she's too worn-out to walk."

John lifted Willa in his arms. She wanted to protest, but she didn't have the strength. Her head lolled against his shoulder. For the first time in months, she felt truly safe, but it was only an illusion. Someone wanted to steal her daughters away. She was their only protection. She couldn't let down her guard.

John waited until his mother pulled back the covers, then he laid Willa gently on the bed in the guest room and took a step back. He hooked his thumbs through his suspenders, feeling ill at ease and restless. This woman brought out his protective instincts and he didn't want to feel responsible for her or for her children. He needed to get back to work. The forge would be cooling by now. He'd have to fire it up again. More time and fuel wasted.

His mother began removing Willa's shoes. "What did she say about pretending to be Amish?"

"She said she was raised Amish but her parents left the church. She wants to return and raise her children in our faith."

"Then we must do what we can for her. Does she have people nearby?"

"Near Hope Springs, I think. That's where she was heading."

"That is a long trip from here with such little ones. Joshua Bowman's wife, Mary, is from there. Perhaps they know each other. Did you tell her she was welcome to spend the night with us?"

"*Nee.* I did not, and why should I? She wants to leave." He didn't want them here another hour, let alone overnight.

His mother made shooing motions with her hands. "Your work will keep, but go if you must. I will see to her. You can keep the *kinder* occupied for me. Outside is best, for I want this young mother to get plenty of rest. I am worried about her babe."

He took a quick step back from the bed. "You think she might give birth here?"

"If the *bobli* wants to come, nothing we do or say will stop it, but there is no sense hurrying his or her arrival for lack of a little rest. Go along. You won't be any help if she does go into labor."

She was right about that. He was a volunteer firefighter along with many of his neighbors, but running into a burning house was not as scary as a woman giving birth. "Call me if you need me."

"I can handle this. Get out from underfoot."

Mamm was a tiny thing and crippled with arthritis

that twisted her hands, but she was still a force to be reckoned with when she set her mind to something.

He found the twins sitting at the table in the kitchen. They watched him warily. He could see subtle differences in their features, but he wasn't sure which was which. Both of them were without their *kapps*. "Come outside and help me with my chores. Your mother is taking a nap."

"Will we see a cow?" The girl closest to him asked.

"Which one are you?"

"Told you. I'm Lucy."

"That's right, you did."

Her sister licked a smear of jam from the back of her hand. "Cows yucky. I'm this many." She held up three fingers.

Lucy nodded and folded her fingers into the correct number. "I'm this many."

Megan pointed to him. "How old are you?"

"Older than all your fingers and toes together."

"I can count. One, two, four, five, three." Lucy ticked off each finger.

"That's very good. Put on your coats. Would you like to feed the goats?"

"Same as at the zoo?" Lucy nodded vigorously.

John had no idea how they fed goats at a zoo, but he figured it couldn't be much different than what he did. He helped Lucy into her coat.

Megan pulled away from him when he tried to help her. "I can do it."

She got her coat on but couldn't manage the buttons. It was getting cold outside, so he buttoned her coat in spite of her protests and held open the door for them when he was done. Megan hung back until Lucy went out, then she hurried after her sister.

"Where's my horsey? Give him back." Megan narrowed her eyes as she looked up at him. She pointed to her mother's buggy sitting beside the barn. He'd fetched it after his mother arrived home and stabled the tired horse.

"I didn't steal her. She is resting in the barn just as your mother is resting in the house."

"What's a barn?" Lucy waited for his answer.

"That big red building."

He figured that was enough information. He was wrong. He wasn't prepared for the barrage of questions a pair of three-year-olds could ask, but he soon learned their curiosity was endless. Most of the time he understood only half of what they were chattering about and he couldn't keep the two of them straight when they darted every which way so quickly.

"Why are cows brown?"

"God made them that color."

"What do cows eat?"

"Hay." He forked some over the stall to his milk cow Maybell.

"What's hay?"

"Dried grass."

"You have a funny hat, Johnjohn."

"It's just John."

"Can cow come in the house?" one asked.

He quickly shook his head. "*Nee*, the cow can't come in the house."

The other child parked her hands on her hips. "Cow come with me!"

"No," he repeated sternly.

A mutinous expression appeared on her face and she shook a finger at him. "Don't tell me no!"

He leaned down to look into her eyes. "No!"

Tears welled up and quickly spilled down her cheeks. "You bad man."

He raised his eyes to the barn ceiling. How did they know at this young age that tears could turn a man's resolve into putty? "I am not bringing a cow into the house."

"I see kitty," one said and ran toward the yellow tabby perched on the window ledge.

Her sister's tears vanished, and she went running toward the animal, too. The cat didn't care for the sudden attention. She jumped down and scampered out the door.

Both children turned toward him. One scowled. "Kitty ran 'way."

"I don't blame her. I'd like to do that myself." He decided the frowning one was Megan and decided to test his theory. "Megan, do you like goats?"

She nodded. Okay, he had that right. "Come, we will feed them now."

He gave each child a pail of grain. His small herd crowded around the children, eager to reach the feed. Lucy petted the head of each goat that came to investigate her. "Me like goats."

"They can't come in the house," he said quickly to forestall another episode of tears.

"Okeydokey," Lucy said.

"Where did you girls come from?" he asked, hoping to get more information about them.

Lucy pointed toward the road.

"What town did you come from?" he asked to be

more specific. He was more curious about their pretty mother than he cared to admit.

Megan sighed deeply. "Our town."

Lucy's lower lip trembled. "Me want to sleep in my bed."

"You will sleep in a warm bed tonight, I promise." He laid a hand on her head. To his surprise, she wrapped her arms around his legs.

She looked up at him. "You nice, Johnjohn."

"No! Bad man," Megan yelled. She yanked Lucy away from him, making Lucy wince at the tight grip on her arm.

John leaned down to frown at Megan. "That was unkind. You must tell your *shveshtah* you are sorry and ask her forgiveness."

For a second he thought she would defy him, but she put her arms around Lucy and pulled her close. "I'm sorry."

Lucy pulled away and sniffled. "It's okay."

John stood up straight. "*Goot.* Your family is second only to God in your life. You must care for each other always. Let's go milk the cow. Maybe your mother will be awake by then and I can get back to work." His first order of business was to see what was wrong with the rear wheels of their buggy. His mother was insistent that they stay overnight, but he wanted them on their way first thing tomorrow.

His attempt to milk the cow proved far more difficult than he had imagined. In spite of his cautions, Lucy tried to catch Maybell's tail as Megan crawled under her belly to see what he was doing. The cow jumped and almost upset his milk pail when Lucy squealed loudly. She had spotted Maybell's twin calves in the next pen.

The girls climbed the wooden fence and jabbered to each other and to the curious calves in a steady stream of words he couldn't hope to keep up with.

They squealed again. He grabbed the pail as the cow kicked nervously. His chores had never been so nerve-racking. A glance over his shoulder revealed five kittens had come out of the hay to get their supper portion of fresh milk. The cats beat a hasty retreat when the girls rushed them.

"Johnjohn, why kitties run away?" Lucy demanded.

"You scared them by being too noisy. You must be quiet around the animals."

"Why?"

"Because all creatures enjoy peace and quiet. Including this blacksmith."

"Kitties!" Megan said, pointing toward the top of the hay bales where the litter had taken refuge.

"Leave them alone, and they will come down." He poured a portion of the milk into a small wooden trough.

He walked to the barn door and held it open. "Come, we must take the *millich* to *Mamm* so we can have fresh cream on our oatmeal tomorrow morning."

They were halfway across the front yard when the door of the house flew open, and Willa came rushing out. Her cheeks were bright red and her eyes were glassy. "I've slept too long. We have to be on our way. Get in the buggy, girls. Where is my horse?"

His mother came out of the house and took hold of Willa's arm. "You are feverish, child. You can't travel today."

"I have to go. You don't understand. I have to go or they will take my babies away from me." She staggered closer to John. "I need a horse. Please, get my horse."

He looked at his mother, and she shook her head. He spoke softly to Willa. "You can't go until you are better. The girls are fine. See?"

He stepped aside so she could see them. "No one is going to take them. They are safe here. Go back into the house, where it's warm."

She clasped her arms across her chest. A shiver racked her body. A second later, her eyes rolled back in her head and she collapsed. He managed to catch her before she hit the ground.

He headed toward the house with her in his arms. By the time he reached the steps, her eyes fluttered open. She pushed against his chest. "I'm fine. Put me down."

"You aren't fine and you aren't going anywhere except back to bed. You will stay there until my mother tells you that you may get up. Is that understood?"

"I need to get to Hope Springs tonight. I can't let the children spend another night on the road." He barely heard her hoarse whisper.

"You can't get to Hope Springs before nightfall. It's a two-day trip from here."

"That can't be."

"Your horse must have carried you many miles out of your way. You can send a letter to your family, telling them that you have been delayed. Or I can use the neighborhood phone and call them if you will give me a number. That way they won't be worrying about you."

She closed her eyes and shook her head. "They aren't expecting me."

He stood aside so his mother could open the door for him. "That's *goot*. They can be just as surprised and happy to see you when you are well. Now, back to bed with you."

She closed her eyes. "You are very bossy."

He fought back a smile. "And you are very stubborn."

"So I have been told," she whispered before her head lolled to the side, and he knew she was asleep again.

She didn't rouse when he laid her on the bed. He stepped back and thrust his hands in his pockets. Her daughters crept in behind him. Lucy tugged on the hem of his coat. "Mama sick?"

Willa looked small and vulnerable lying beneath the thick quilt. He wanted to see her standing strong with that stubborn chin jutting out. He nodded. "*Ja*, I think she is very sick."

Megan squeezed past him, grasped her mother's hand and tugged on it. "Mama get up."

His mother scowled at him and leaned down to reassure Megan, slipping her arm around the child's shoulders. "Your *mamm* just needs to rest. *Kumm*, we must let her sleep. You are all going to stay with us for a few days. Won't that be nice?"

"Feed cows again?" Lucy asked.

"*Ja*. Tomorrow John will let you feed all the animals again. Now it's time to make our own supper. Go into the kitchen. I'll be there in a minute. You may each have a cookie from the plate that is on the counter."

The girls reluctantly left the bedroom. John followed his mother down the hall. "You sound positively delighted to have this family of strangers stay on for days."

"I am."

"Well, I'm not. I haven't been able to get a single piece of work done today."

She stopped and turned to face him. "You have done nothing but work yourself half to death for the past four years."

"You speak as if that is a poor thing."

"Work is all well and good, but you've forgotten how to have a little fun now and again."

"I know how to have fun." His mother was being ridiculous.

"What was the last thing you did simply for the fun of it?" She stared at him with her arms crossed.

"I enjoy my work. It is fun to me."

"You can't think of anything, can you?"

He shook his finger at her. "If they do stay another day, you will keep the chatterboxes occupied while I get caught up on my work. A forge is no place for such wild *kinder.*"

"They aren't wild."

"Maybell will disagree with you."

"I will keep them. All you had to do was ask." She smiled sweetly, and he saw exactly how tomorrow was going to turn out. It would be a repeat of today.

"The first thing on my list will be repairing their buggy so they can leave."

"If *Gott* wishes them to go, they will go. If He wishes them to stay, they will stay." His mother turned away and walked into the kitchen.

Chapter Four

Willa stretched her stiff and aching muscles, then snuggled down beneath the warm quilt again, reluctant to open her eyes. If only she could stay asleep for a few more minutes. Just a few more.

"You're awake, I see."

The familiar voice put an end to Willa's wishful thinking. She turned her head and found John's mother sitting in a rocker beside the bed. There was daylight pouring through the window. "What time is it?"

Pushing to her feet, Vera patted Willa's shoulder. "Time to eat something. I'll be back in a minute with your tray. I hope you like strong tea. I never could drink coffee while I was pregnant."

"You don't need to coddle me," Willa said, but Vera was already out the door.

Willa sat up in bed and pushed her hair back from her face. Her chest ached from coughing and her throat was scratchy, but she didn't intend to stay in bed another day as much as she wished she could.

"This is not coddling. It's plain common sense," Vera said as she returned with a tray of tea and cinnamon toast. "The more you rest, the sooner you will be well enough to travel. Perhaps tomorrow."

When Vera finished propping pillows behind Willa, she placed the tray on her lap.

Willa smiled her thanks. "A good night's sleep has done wonders for me. I won't trouble you any longer."

"Eat and then we shall see."

"Where are my daughters?" Willa looked past Vera to the empty hall. She wasn't used to having the girls out of her sight. She couldn't rest easy until she saw them.

"They are helping my son John with the chores. I believe they are gathering the eggs and feeding the chickens."

Willa bit her lower lip. "I'm not sure they will be much help."

Vera chuckled. "I'm sure you are right, but John needs a lesson in patience. *Kinder* are often the best teachers of that virtue."

"I don't want them to annoy him."

Vera moved to the window to look out. "I hope they will. My son has become a stuffy fellow. It will do him good to see the world through the eyes of little ones for a change."

Willa moved the food tray aside. The last thing she wanted was to cause John trouble. He'd been more than kind. "I can't thank you enough for all you've done for us, but I must be going. I still have a long way to travel. Has John had a chance to repair my buggy?"

Willa stood. The room spun wildly. She closed her eyes and pressed a hand to her head as Vera steadied her.

"Sit before you fall down."

"It will pass. I stood up too quickly, that's all."

"*Nee*, this is your babe's way of saying you need

more rest. Back in bed and don't try getting up again unless John or I am close by. I don't want to have to pick you up off the floor."

Willa's legs trembled, forcing her to sit on the side of the bed. As much as she hated to admit it, she wasn't going anywhere until she had regained more of her strength. She meekly allowed Vera to tuck her in again. When the dizziness subsided, Willa opened her eyes to find Vera watching her with a worried expression. It had been a long time since anyone had worried over her.

"I'm fine now. Truly I am."

"You will drink your tea and eat your toast, and not another word about leaving. Is that understood?"

"It is," Willa answered, feeling like a scolded child. Vera Miller was clearly used to giving orders and being obeyed.

"*Goot.* Rest today and tomorrow you will feel much better."

After Vera left the room, Willa sipped the tea and nibbled on the toast as she took stock of her situation. She couldn't leave today, and it wouldn't do her any good to argue. She shuddered to think what could have happened yesterday when her horse was trotting unguided along the roads. They were safe for now. The children were being fed and looked after, something she couldn't do herself.

Leaning back against the headboard, she drew a deep breath, pleased that it didn't trigger a coughing fit. The tea was soothing, and it was making her sleepy.

Another day's rest would see her stronger, but she couldn't stay longer than that. Time was growing short. She had to learn if her great-aunt or her cousins would take her and the children in. Her baby was due in less than two months. She had to have a safe place for the girls and her babe before she gave birth. Nothing mattered but protecting them, even from herself.

"How is she?" John asked his mother when he came in. His two terrors followed right behind him. He hoped Willa Lapp was able to travel. Keeping an eye on her two energetic children was exhausting. How did women do it? Between answering their endless questions and keeping them out of harm's way, he was ready to cart them all to Hope Springs himself.

"Willa is resting at the moment, but she is in no shape to travel. She stood at the side of the bed and almost fainted."

He stifled a groan. That wasn't what he wanted to hear. He wanted her to be on her way, but he could hardly push a sick woman out the door. "Then the *kinder* must stay with you the rest of the day. I have work to do and I cannot have them underfoot. They court disaster at every turn."

His mother frowned at him. "That's a harsh thing to say about such darlings."

"Johnjohn's mad," Lucy told her.

John pointed at her. "This one almost tumbled out of the hayloft door. I barely caught her in time. Megan dropped the basket of eggs and broke half of them. And someone left the henhouse door open. I spent the last hour hunting down and catching our chickens."

His mother actually smiled, making him feel foolish for allowing two children to get the better of him. "I wondered what was taking so long. Accidents happen. It's not as if they are going out of their way to annoy

you, but I will keep them with me for the rest of the day. Does that make you happy?"

"It does. Very, very happy."

"*Kumm* and *redd-up*, girls."

Megan cocked her head to the side. "What's *redd-up*?"

"It means to clean up. I can't believe John let you get so dirty."

His mouth dropped open. "I let them? I don't know how I could stop them. They crawl under and over and into everything."

"Never mind. A little dirt washes off easily enough. Shall we go in and see your *mamm*? She's been missing you."

"I miss Mama. Need a hug." Megan followed his mother to the kitchen sink and allowed her to wipe her dirty hands and face.

Lucy stood beside him, looking up with sad eyes. "Johnjohn mad at me?"

He blew out a cleansing breath. "*Nee*, I'm not mad at you. Go wash your face."

She smiled brightly. "Okeydokey."

When she wasn't being a bother, she had an engaging way about her. He watched as his mother led them down the hall to the guest room. He had plenty of work waiting but found himself following them instead. He wanted to see for himself that Willa couldn't travel. He wouldn't put it past his mother to keep her abed just to annoy him.

From the doorway he saw Willa propped up in bed. She had her eyes closed, and it looked as though she were sleeping. She was pale with dark circles under her eyes and bright spots of color in her cheeks. Was she still running a fever? Guilt replaced his annoyance. She did look ill.

Her eyes opened as her daughters climbed onto the bed with her. The transformation on her face was amazing. He had seldom seen such radiant joy. It was as if the sun had come out after a fierce storm.

She stretched out her arms and pulled the girls to her sides. "This is what I need to make me feel better. Lovebug hugs."

She gave her affection so freely. He wasn't used to seeing that. Most Amish women were very reserved. Public displays of affection were frowned upon.

Willa caught sight of him. "I hope they haven't been troubling you, John."

"Not a bit." He shoved his hands in his pockets, unsure why he didn't tell her the truth.

"They can be a handful. Two handfuls." She kissed each child on the head. "I see you have your *kapps* on. That's good."

"Where yours?" Megan asked.

Willa brushed a strand of her hair back from her face and looked around. "I'm not sure. Where is my dignity?"

Her tousled curls caught the sunlight shining in and glowed with a warm light that made him want to stretch his hand out and touch them. It wasn't proper for a man to see a woman with her head uncovered. A woman's hair was her crowning glory, meant to be seen only by God and by her husband.

"Here it is," John said, picking up the covering where it had fallen to the floor. He handed it to her, looking away in embarrassment as she finger combed her hair and settled the *kapp* on her head. He shoved his hands in his pockets again.

"Johnjohn's mad at me," Lucy said with a pout and a mournful look in his direction.

"He is? What did you do?" Willa asked.

Lucy cupped a hand to her mother's ear and whispered loudly. "I let the chickies go bye-bye. I'm sorry."

"Oh, dear. I'm sure John has forgiven you. You won't do it again, will you?"

Lucy solemnly shook her head. "Megan broked the eggs."

"On accident." Megan glared at him.

Willa clapped a hand over her mouth. "Oh, John, I'm sorry. You have had your hands full."

He shrugged. "They didn't mean any harm."

"Of course they didn't," his mother said as she slipped past him with a sly grin on her face.

"Rest up," he said to Willa, backing away. "Your horse is fine, and I'll have your buggy fixed in no time."

"Thank you, John. Girls, why don't you stay with me for a little while?"

"Play games?" Megan asked with a bright smile. "Hide-and-seek?"

"Not today. Lucy, there is a book in my backpack on the floor by the window. Will you bring it here, please?"

"I'll get it," John said, quickly crossing the floor. He grasped the backpack by the strap and laid it on the bed beside her.

"Thank you, John. Lucy, you pick the first story. Megan, you can pick the second one. Okay?"

The girls nodded. Lucy peered into the bag and pulled out a tattered children's book. "This one."

"The story about the kitten who lost her mittens. We like this one, don't we?"

Lucy nodded vigorously. "We saw kitties. They runned away."

"Sometimes it takes a while for kittens to learn to like a new person. If you are kind to them, they will soon warm up to you."

"Bad man scared them," Megan said.

John was shocked to see fear widen Willa's eyes. "What bad man? Did you see him?" she demanded.

Megan pointed to John. "Him."

Willa visibly relaxed. "John isn't a bad man. He's a nice fellow."

Megan frowned. "Nice?"

"Very nice." Willa glanced at him and quickly looked away.

He couldn't be sure, but he thought she might be blushing.

Megan didn't look as if she believed her mother.

John pondered Willa's reaction to Megan's words as he walked back to the kitchen. His mother was busy mixing something in a bowl. He checked the stove and found there was still coffee in the pot. He poured himself a cup and leaned his hip against the counter. "Has Willa told you much about herself?"

"*Nee*, and I haven't asked. Why?"

"Something Megan said. She said the bad man scared the kittens. She meant me, but I saw fear on Willa's face."

His mother stopped stirring. "What do you think it means?"

"I don't know. Maybe she is running away from someone."

She started stirring again. "I don't like to think that, but I reckon it's possible."

"Yesterday she said someone was trying to take her babies away."

"She had a high fever, John. She might have been out of her head."

"Maybe, but her fear was real." He took a sip of coffee and grimaced. It was cold.

"What can we do about it?" his mother asked.

He walked to the sink and poured out his cup. "I'm going to fix her buggy so she can leave. We don't need outsider problems."

"I will see what I can find out. If she is in trouble, we must help her."

"If she is in trouble, she must take it with her when she leaves," he insisted. She and her children had disrupted his life enough.

"I don't know how I raised such a hard-hearted man. Your wife would have wanted to help this poor woman."

He cringed inwardly. "Katie's gone."

"So is your father, but you and I are here until *Gott* calls *us* home. What we do with the rest of our lives is important. Hiding in your smithy isn't the way God wants you to live. You are young. You still have time to find love, a wife, a family, if only you would open your heart."

"I tried it your way, remember? It didn't work out."

"Your father and I pressured you to court Rebecca, I admit as much. That was a mistake on our part. It was too soon for you, but because Rebecca loved another is no reason for you to give up on finding happiness."

"I'm happy enough. I don't need a wife. I had one and God took her from me. What I need is to get back to work." He stormed out of the kitchen, slamming the door behind him.

Chapter Five

Willa cupped her hands over her belly as her baby kicked hard enough to make her wince. "Please don't be in a hurry to arrive," she whispered. "If you give me enough time, I promise to make sure you are safe. I love you so much already."

She looked up to see Vera standing in the doorway. "Is everything all right? I thought I heard the front door slam."

"My son gets tired of my prodding ways and balks like a stubborn mule at times. At least when he does, I know he is paying attention to my ramblings."

"Is he upset because we are here?"

Vera dismissed her suggestion with a wave of her hand. "All things in the world are by the will of *Gott*. You are here because He wishes it. My son will come to that conclusion in time."

Willa smoothed a wrinkle from the cover over her lap. She needed to believe God would protect her, but doubts crept in when she was alone. "I want to believe in His great goodness, but sometimes I wonder how He can allow such sadness in the world."

"His ways are beyond our understanding. His plan is too large for us to see more than a tiny portion of it, but He has a plan for us all."

"Mama, more story." Lucy pushed the book toward Willa.

"In a minute, darling."

Vera sat on the edge of the bed. "I happen to have a box of toys in my bedroom across the hall. It's a big brown wooden box under the window. Would you girls like to look for something to play with? I'm sure I have a doll for each of you in there."

"Yeah." Megan slid off the bed and Lucy quickly followed her.

Vera watched them go and then turned to Willa. "What kind of trouble are you in?"

Taken aback by Vera's bluntness, Willa tried to stall until she could decide what to say. "Why do you ask that?"

"So you *are* in trouble."

"I didn't say I was."

"You didn't say you weren't. Tell me about it. I want to help."

"I'm not— It's not— It's nothing that involves you." Willa stared out the window.

"John and I will help if we can."

Willa looked at the kindly face of the woman beside her. "I believe you would. If there was a way for you to help me, I would tell you, but there isn't anything you can do."

"I could be the judge of that if I knew what was wrong. What are you afraid of? Is it your husband? Not all men are kind."

"My husband was a gentle man. He'd never hurt anyone."

"So who brings the fear to your eyes that my son says he has seen?"

John was more perceptive than Willa expected. Maybe it was because she was still so tired, but she found she needed to confide in someone. "If you must know, my husband's parents want to take my daughters away from me. They say I'm an unfit mother."

Vera drew back. "How can they do such a thing?"

"They have money and influence. They say the law is on their side. I'm not a bad mother. I'm not." She was too ashamed to tell Vera about her past illness. Tears welled up in Willa's eyes. It all seemed so hopeless. She couldn't even get out of bed, let alone protect those dearest to her.

"The *Englisch* lawmen look for you, also?"

Willa nodded.

"Is this why you are pretending to be Amish?"

"I didn't know what else to do. I had very little money. I bought bus tickets for us to the town near where my grandfather has a farm. I got off before we reached it. That is where I first met John."

Vera's eyes widened. "You have met my son before?"

"Just once. It was after we left the bus. He was kind enough to give us a ride on his wagon so the girls didn't have to walk so far."

"I wonder that he didn't mention this," Vera said more to herself than to Willa. "Why didn't you stay with your *daddi*?"

Willa looked away. "Grandfather wouldn't take us in. He didn't believe that I wanted to become Amish again. He said I should have returned sooner."

"That is shameful. We are to welcome those who wish to return to us. The Lord will judge his actions one day. He should remember that."

Willa gave her a watery smile. "Don't think too harshly of him. He gave us these Amish clothes and told me to go to his sister, who lives near Hope Springs. He said if I truly repent and join the faith, I may return to him."

"At least he had some kindness for you. Will your great-aunt take you in?"

"I don't know." Willa's voice broke. She pressed her hands to her mouth to hold back a sob. Crying wouldn't help. It never helped.

Vera sighed heavily. "This is a difficult situation. It will take much prayer to see the path our Lord wishes us to follow. It is not right to keep your *kinder* from their grandparents, but I understand why you feel you must. Have you spoken with them? Are you sure of their intentions?"

"My husband spoke to them. He told me he couldn't change their minds. They have a man searching for us, a private detective. He was always able to find us, and each time we were forced to move again. I don't know how he found us in Columbus, but he did. I went out to buy some milk for the girls, and when I came back to the apartment, the woman next door said the police and this man had been there looking for me. She had promised to call them when I returned, but she said she didn't promise to call them right away." Willa laughed at the memory of the elderly Mrs. Kramer's daring, but her laugh held an edge of hysteria. She had come so close to losing her babies.

She thanked God for a half gallon of milk and the

unconventional spirited old woman who had lived beside them. In some ways, Vera reminded Willa of Mrs. Kramer. She had the same sharp look in her aged eyes. "You and your son have been kind to me, as well. I can never repay you."

"Your prayers for us are repayment enough. God moves in strange ways, but He has brought you here for a reason," Vera muttered.

She stood and laid a hand on Willa's cheek. "This detective will not find you. We Amish are in the world, but we are not a part of this world. We have our own ways and they serve us well, for we serve *Gott* first."

"I hope and pray he doesn't find us. I have to believe my great-aunt will help. I want my children to celebrate this Christmas and many more with my family."

"One of the Bowman sons is married to a woman from Hope Springs. She may know your family. This man is looking for an *Englisch* woman and her daughters, *ja*?"

"He is."

Vera patted Willa's arm. "Get some rest. No one will take your *kinder* while you sleep. There is only an Amish *frau* and her daughters visiting us if anyone should ask."

Willa rubbed her face with both hands. "I'm afraid we won't pass for Amish if anyone looks closely."

"Then no one must look closely. In time you will become more Amish and so will your little ones."

Time wasn't on Willa's side, but her daughters were safe for now. Her body and mind craved rest. She snuggled down under the quilt again. She heard Megan and Lucy arguing over a doll in the other room, but before she could get up, Vera intervened and the squabble ended.

What would John make of Willa's story when his mother filled him in on the details? She knew Vera would tell him. Among the Amish, the man was the head of the house. All important decisions were made by men. Women had their say, to be sure, but it would be up to John to allow Willa to stay or to inform the police of her whereabouts.

It was a relief to have that much of her past out in the open, but she didn't dare try to explain why Glen's family feared for the children's welfare. Willa wouldn't hurt them, not knowingly, but what might happen if the voices came back after her baby was born? Someone had to keep them safe if she wasn't able to care for them. The Amish valued God first, family second and then the community. They cared for their own. She prayed her great-aunt's family would provide all she needed.

John came in from the outside and wiped his feet on the mat. His mother was standing beside the table staring at him with a deep frown etched between her brows. She tapped one foot as she waited for him to speak. Whatever she was upset about, he was sure it was something to do with that woman. The one he couldn't stop thinking about. The one with golden curls who gave lovebug kisses.

"I know that look, *Mamm*. What is on your mind?"

"Why didn't you tell me you had met Willa before?"

"It didn't seem important." He took off his coat and hung up his hat. When he looked her way, she hadn't moved.

"Not important? The Lord places this stranger, this

desperate young mother, into your care twice in a single week, and you don't think that is important enough to mention?"

"I admit it is a strange coincidence, but that's all. She's leaving. Her own family will take care of her as soon as she reaches them. What's for lunch?"

"Don't change the subject."

"The subject of that woman and her children is closed. Her buggy has been repaired. Her horse is rested, but the poor creature isn't up to a long trip. I will send the family on their way with one of our horses."

"You have more concern for an animal than you do for that poor child. She is not up to a long journey, either."

"What do you want me to do? She needs to be with her own family during this time. I can't spare four days away from my work to drive her to Hope Springs and then drive back. I'm not going to pay for a driver to take her. We can't afford it."

"You may be right about that."

He hadn't expected her to give in. "I am."

"She can write to her family and ask if they will send the money. In the meantime, she can get plenty of rest and regain her strength, and I will have the chance to enjoy her darling daughters. It shouldn't take more than a week."

"*Mamm, I* don't want her here."

"And why is that?"

Did he have to spell it out? He clenched his jaw until his teeth ached. If his mother needed the hard truth, he would give it. "She's a reminder."

"A reminder of what?" his mother asked gently.

"That Katie and I could have given you grandchildren

by now if God had spared her life. She is a reminder of how unfair life is."

"My poor son, I know your grief is deep. So is mine. So is Willa's. Life seems unfair because we do not understand God's great plan for us. We grieve and that is as it should be, but life must be more than grief and sorrow. If that is all you look for, that is all you will find."

She was wrong. He wanted to feel anything but this crushing sorrow. There simply wasn't room in his heart for joy. Willa and her daughters were painful reminders of that fact every time he saw them.

He wasn't narrow-minded enough to think he was the only person to have suffered the loss of a loved one. His mother didn't need to point that out. He pitied Willa, for her loss was as great as his. How did she face each new day? How did she find the strength to get out of bed each morning? Was it because of her daughters? It was something he'd never be able to ask her.

In truth, he didn't want to know anything else about her. He didn't want to feel sorry for her or know she struggled as hard as he did to keep his feelings hidden. He didn't want to like her children or listen to Lucy tell him "okeydokey" with that silly, adorable grin on her face. He didn't want Megan to like him even a little. He wanted to be left alone.

He yanked his coat off the hook and put it on, then jammed his hat on his head. "Don't worry about making me anything for supper. I'll be in the workshop. I parked Willa's buggy close to the house. Make whatever preparations you need to see that they can travel comfortably, but they are leaving in the morning."

John pulled open the door without waiting for his mother to reply. A few snowflakes drifted lazily down around him. The weather forecast in the newspaper that morning had called for occasional flurries. Hopefully it wouldn't amount to much, and his guest could leave as planned.

He spent the next six hours sweating over his forge and shaping the lantern housings he needed for Melvin's sleigh. He finally managed to finish one he was happy with. He should have known better than to try to work when his mind was filled with thoughts of Willa and her problems. At his current rate of speed, it would take him a full year to finish all the work the new sleigh needed. He was bone tired and hungry. He took a deep breath and prepared to go in. He was sure his mother would be waiting up for him. She would be asleep in her chair in the living room, but she never failed to wake up when the door opened.

Opening his workshop door, he saw a light layer of snow coated everything. Streams of it snaked across the ground in the wind and piled up against the side of the buildings, but it wasn't falling at the moment. Willa's buggy sat near the front gate, topped with a white crown. He took the time to brush it off before he went in.

To his surprise, his mother wasn't waiting up. He had braced himself for another argument for no reason. He found a plate of roast beef sandwiches in the refrigerator along with a slice of pumpkin pie topped with fresh whipped cream. It was his favorite. He chuckled as he recognized his mother's way of apologizing.

On his way to bed, he passed his mother's bedroom door and heard the sound of her snoring. He paused outside Willa's door to listen but didn't hear any movement within. He opened the next door softly and looked inside. His mother had made up two cots for the twins, but they were both asleep in one bed with their arms around each other. He closed the door and went to his room at the end of the hall. In spite of his fatigue, he barely slept. A little before six o'clock he rose and got dressed. His mother was in the kitchen. The smell of coffee and frying bacon filled the morning.

Willa sat at the table with a white mug in her hands. She blushed and looked down when she caught sight of him. "Good morning, John."

"Guder mariye," he muttered. She looked more rested, but he couldn't say she looked well. There were still dark shadows beneath her eyes and a hollow look to her cheeks.

"We will be on our way as soon as we have finished eating. Hurry up, girls."

"I'm done," Lucy announced, holding both hands in the air.

John waited for his mother to make some comment, but she didn't. He put on his hat, determined not to feel like he was tossing a bird with a broken wing out into the snow. "I'll hitch up the horse."

Outside, he brought out his best and gentlest buggy horse, a black mare named Clover. She was reliable and steady in traffic. He backed her into place and hitched her to the buggy. He turned to see his mother coming out of the house with a wicker hamper over her arm. Lucy followed her, chatting away and skipping. His mother put the basket down and motioned to him. "Give me a hand with this, John. It's heavy."

His mother was probably sending a week's worth of food with the family for a two-day trip. He started to lead Clover toward her when he heard a loud crack.

Clover jumped forward. The front wheels of the buggy pulled completely out from under it. The cab toppled to the ground as he looked on in astonishment.

Lucy clapped both hands to her cheeks. "Oh, no! Johnjohn broked it!"

His mother smothered a laugh. "He certainly did."

"This isn't funny." He struggled to control the confused horse.

"Lucy, go back inside and tell your *mamm* that you'll all be staying a little longer."

"Okeydokey." Lucy whirled around and ran into the house.

His mother looked up and held out one hand. "I do believe it's beginning to snow."

Chapter Six

"So this is where you've been hiding."

Willa stepped inside John's workshop and shook the snow from her shawl. It had been coming down heavily since early morning, big fat flakes that stuck to everything and piled up fast. Warmth surrounded her inside the building with a low ceiling and tools of John's trade everywhere. The smell of smoke and hot metal filled the air. She peeled off her gloves and tucked them in the pockets of her apron.

John sat at a small desk near the south-facing window with an open ledger book in front of him. "I'm not hiding."

"Perhaps not, but I feel as though we have driven you out of your own house." Willa tightened the black shawl across her shoulders. He hadn't come in since her buggy came apart that morning. The buggy pieces had been moved into the barn, but John hadn't offered any information on the repairs that were needed or how long it might take. Vera had sent Willa to check on him as it was almost time for supper. It was easy to see he didn't want their continued company, but she and the girls wouldn't be able to travel until her vehicle was fixed. Maybe not even then if the snow kept up much longer.

He closed the book he had been writing in. "I've had a lot of work to catch up on, that's all."

"Have you fixed our buggy?"

"Not yet. I seem to be missing the exact parts I need. I'm sure I had some of the same size carriage bolts last week. I can't imagine where they have gone."

"Can't you make some?"

"Not easily. They have to be the right size down to the millimeter."

She looked around the room. Horseshoes of every size hung from pegs on one wall. Assorted tools were lined up in a metal rack. A huge anvil stood near the furnace. The forge itself was a brick structure that resembled a large table with a hood over it and which had a depression where a low fire burned. At the rear of the building were open wooden shelves that held stacks of long steel rods. "I'm afraid I don't know much about the blacksmith trade. A blacksmith's shop is called a smithy, am I right?"

"You are." He busied himself choosing a round steel rod from the stack.

"I see you use coal for your fire. Why not propane? Vera mentioned your church approves the use of some propane appliances and generators."

"A few blacksmiths use propane. I prefer coal or coke as it is called. I get better heat and a coke forge has an advantage because it can be scaled easily."

"What does that mean?"

"It means I can make the fire larger or smaller depending upon my needs."

She moved closer to the forge, where a bed of coal

glowed bright red. She had to take a step back as the heat scorched her face. "How hot does it get?"

"Very hot. About fourteen hundred degrees, but there are times when I need it hotter or colder."

"Hotter than fourteen hundred degrees?"

"Welding requires more heat."

"No wonder you don't allow the girls out here. Lucy is quite brokenhearted that she can't watch you work."

"It's too dangerous. Her pouting will not sway me."

She walked over to the anvil and ran her fingers along the curved surface. "Thank you for that. It must feel good to pound away your frustrations out here."

"If I am frustrated, I clean my shop and go do something else. A clear mind means good work. If I make something when I'm distracted, it often goes in the scrap barrel for another day." He gestured toward a fifty-gallon drum in the corner.

She saw a number of metal pieces sticking out of it. "I hope we are not the cause of these failed projects."

He ignored her comment. "Blacksmithing is about control, not about power or strength. Sometimes I must hit the metal hard, but it is more important to hit the metal as accurately as I can. When I first started working beside my father in this shop, he drew an X on the anvil. He said, 'Strike here only. Move your work, not your hammer. Chasing it around the anvil will result in a ruined piece.' He was right."

"It sounds difficult to me."

"Like everything worthwhile, it comes with time and practice."

"What happens if you make a mistake?"

"There are no mistakes."

It was her turn to smile. "Are you that good?"

He shook his head. "Metal can be reused. If I botch a piece, I simply give it another chance as something else." He crossed to the forge and pumped the bellows, making the coals glow hotter.

"What are you making today?"

"Cabinet pulls. I sell them at Luke Bowman's hardware store. He has ordered twenty of them."

"Will it annoy you if I watch?"

He shrugged. "I don't mind."

"Explain to me what you are doing?" He definitely seemed more relaxed out here among his tools.

"A blacksmith needs four basic things. A way to heat his work. A way to hold his work. Something to put under his work and a way to apply forces to his work."

"Let me guess. The forge is for heating things."

A smile tugged at the corner of his mouth. "Very *goot*. I heat my work with a forge. Forges need fuel and air, lots of air, hence the bellows."

She gestured to the array of long-handled tools. "These pincher things are for holding your work."

"Tongs, and you're half right. I hold things with tongs but also with vises or clamps. There are a number of different tongs for holding various shapes."

He picked one up. "This tong is made for holding a half-inch square rod, but it won't work if I try to hold a round rod. A flat piece of stock requires that one." He pointed to the tong on the end. "I have to be able to hold tight to the hot steel when I hit it. A good vise is also an important tool. Not a cheap one that you can buy in an *Englisch* store, but one made for heavy-duty work."

She patted the anvil. "I assume since this is bolted down that it goes under your hot metal."

"Right once again. This is a finely designed tool.

It also belonged to my father. You'll notice it has two holes in it. They are called the pritchel and the hardy hole. A pritchel is used for punching through a piece of metal. It also holds the work steady so it doesn't distort when I start punching. The hardy holds cold tools. I use a V-block to put a bend in a piece or make a curved shape. The horn, the pointy end of the anvil, is used for curving metal around it."

It was much more information than Willa really wanted to know, but she was interested because he was interested. She could tell it was more than his job. It was his passion.

He brought a length of steel rod to the table and placed one end in the fire. In a matter of minutes, he had cut the glowing metal into several shorter lengths. Then he twisted them into a spiral pattern and punched out the screw holes for a set of nearly identical cabinet pull handles.

"You make it look easy."

"A piece this size is easy."

"So you say. Thank you for the demonstration. It was very interesting." She picked up several of the horseshoes. "My husband would have loved this place," she said softly.

"What did he do? Does it bother you to talk about him?" he added quickly.

She smiled softly. "Talking about Glen doesn't bother me. He was an amazing person in my life. I can't pretend he didn't exist because he's gone now. The pain of his loss is with me if I talk about him or not. Does that make sense?"

"It does."

"Glen didn't have a craft the way you do. His passion

was horses. Funny, isn't it? He wasn't Amish, but he loved working around the trotters and pacers we use to pull our buggies. Whenever we had to move, he always went to the local racetracks to find a job. He could talk for hours about this horse's stats or why that horse's jockey wasn't the best fit. And horseshoes. He knew a lot about horseshoes and how they make a horse run better, the same way a good pair of track shoes makes a human sprinter run faster."

She noticed John watching her closely. "I'm sorry. I haven't had anyone I could talk to about Glen since he died. The girls won't remember him in a few years. I don't know how to keep his memory alive for them except through my memories. He went out to the corner store to pick up a loaf of bread because I had forgotten to get some that afternoon."

She had just learned she was pregnant after a visit to the local free clinic. She'd been too upset to remember the bread. She'd never got up the nerve to tell Glen he was going to be a father again.

"What happened?"

There was so much compassion in John's voice that it brought tears to her eyes. She turned away so he wouldn't see them. "He was struck and killed by a speeding car as he crossed the street. They never found the driver."

"You miss him." It was a statement of fact, not a question. She appreciated that.

She took a deep breath. "I do. Every day. Just as I know you must miss your wife."

He nodded. "As you say, every day."

Willa saw the pain in his eyes and wanted to offer any comfort she could. "What was she like? I know the

Amish don't normally talk about the loved ones they have lost, but I'm willing to listen."

A hint of a smile touched his lips. "She was a little like you."

"Like me how? Short with blond hair and big feet?"

"*Nee*, she was tall and willowy with thick glossy brown hair and gray-green eyes, and I don't think you have big feet."

"Then why do you say she was like me?"

"She had your…attitude. I think that is the word I want."

"What kind of attitude do I have?" She expected him to say small and timid.

"I've seen you stick out your chin like you are daring the world to stand in your way."

His answer surprised her. "My husband called it my stubborn streak."

"*Ja*. That's exactly what I called Katie's attitude when she wanted something done her way. I think she would have liked you, Willa Lapp."

It was an unexpected compliment. "It's a shame you didn't have children. They make it easier sometimes. When I want to lie down and weep, I can't because I have to take care of my girls."

The smile vanished from his face. He stared at the fire in his forge. "Katie was pregnant with our first child when she was killed."

Willa pressed a hand to her chest. Her heart actually ached for him. There were no words to express her sympathy, so she remained quiet. The only sounds were the crackle of the fire and the moaning wind rising outside.

After a few moments, John spoke again. "We had an argument that afternoon. She wanted to go to an ice-skating party with some of our friends. I thought it was a bad idea. I forbade it. She ignored me. She hitched up her pony cart and drove away. I should have stopped her. I should have reasoned with her instead of putting my foot down. I knew how stubborn she could be."

He held his hand toward the fire. "I should have gone with her. Her cart was struck by a pickup at the end of our lane. I saw it happening, and I couldn't do anything to stop it."

Drawn to his pain, Willa stepped close and gently pulled his hand away from the heat. "I'm sorry. It is a terrible thing to endure."

John fastened his gaze on her small fingers where they rested on his arm. She didn't tell him it was God's will. She didn't say his wife and child were in a better place and that he would see them again if he lived a devout life. He didn't want to hear those words. He'd heard them so often they no longer held any meaning.

Willa simply said she was sorry. She understood—he felt it in the gentle touch of her hand. She didn't make light of his pain or his guilt. How could this stranger understand him so well?

His mother had lost a son and her husband of forty years not long afterward, but she carried on. He knew her grief was real—he grieved for them, too—but she faced it differently. He didn't have his mother's strength. Maybe he didn't have her faith.

He looked at Willa. "You should get back to the house. *Mamm* will start to worry about you if you are gone too long. The weather is getting worse. You might not be traveling for a day or two even after I fix your buggy."

"I'm sorry you are stuck with us, but we will be

leaving sooner or later. I need to reach my great-aunt and her family before this baby arrives." Her expression grew somber, and he wondered why. He thought all mothers looked forward to the arrival of their children with joy.

"Is everything okay with your babe?"

She placed a hand on her belly and rubbed in slow circles. "I pray it is. I pray every day and night."

He longed to chase the worry from her eyes and reassure her. "God hears your prayers, and He will answer them."

"I know." She looked up and smiled. "Your mother wants you to come in for supper. I'm to drag you there by the ear if I must."

He laughed. "I would like to see you try. You're no bigger than a mouse."

She flexed her arm. "I have more muscle than you think. Don't forget, I've been picking up two toddlers for ages. That's a workout. Hammering a horseshoe is nothing compared to the strength it takes to stop Lucy from bolting. Hauling you in by the ear would be a piece of cake compared to managing those two."

"I won't put you to the test, although I might challenge you to arm wrestle in the future just to prove you wrong."

"Not on an empty stomach, please. I'm starving. Come in the house."

"As soon as I've put out my fire."

"I'll wait for you." She raised the heavy shawl over her head and pulled on her gloves.

A familiar beeping broke the stillness in the room.

"What is that?" Willa asked.

"My pager." He pulled the device from the waistband of his pants and read the scrolling message it displayed.

"Blacksmiths need pagers?"

"They do if they are part of the volunteer fire department," he said.

"Is there a fire?"

"*Nee*, it was only a message telling me they have rescheduled our meeting with the county emergency management folks for Saturday afternoon."

"That's a blessing. It would be rough weather to fight a fire."

"There is no good weather for a fire." He clipped the pager back on his waistband and tidied his shop. After making sure the fire was out, he held the door open for Willa. A fierce gust of wind hit, knocking her back against him. He caught her by the shoulders and steadied her. He could barely make out the light from the window across the way. "Take care. This is worse than I thought."

She turned her face away from the wind. "I can't see the house. We might become lost if we go out into this."

He grasped her gloved hand. "We won't. I can see the light in the kitchen window. Hang on to me. I don't want us to get separated."

She tucked her chin into the folds of the shawl. "Promise you won't let go."

He squeezed her hand. "I promise. You are safe with me."

She tightened her grip and nodded. "I trust you, John Miller."

Willa woke the next morning to the sound of the wind roaring outside and snow hissing against the window in her bedroom. The storm was still in progress. She smiled as she sat up, feeling more rested than she had in ages. No one would find her today.

Her son or daughter kicked against her ribs, making her sit up straighter. She smiled and patted her belly. "Someone else is feeling better, too."

Her stomach rumbled, and Willa realized she was famished. "Maybe you're trying to tell me you are hungry. You're going to be a roly-poly little thing if we stay here much longer. Vera's roasted chicken and biscuits last night were the best I've ever had."

Tossing back the quilt, she slipped out of bed and dressed quickly in the cold room, grateful for the woolen leggings Vera had loaned her. Willa paused to pray that her own family would be as welcoming and as kind as the Millers had been.

After checking on her daughters and finding them sleeping, Willa made her way to the kitchen by lamplight. The rest of the house was quiet. Neither John nor Vera appeared to be up yet. Willa lowered the chain that held the pair of ceiling lamps and lit their mantles with long matches from a holder on the wall. She raised the lamps again and a warm glow illuminated the room.

Rubbing her hands together to warm them, she turned her attention to food and began rummaging through the kitchen cupboards and refrigerator. She came up with the ingredients for a Spanish omelet. She hummed as she whipped the eggs, diced the potatoes and dried peppers, and heated the oil in a skillet. It was wonderful to be free of worry—at least for a day.

She had shelter and warmth, her daughters were sleeping snug in their beds and she had the run of a well-stocked kitchen. It had been so long since she'd had these most basic elements that she refused to think about what the future held and simply enjoyed the moment.

She was slipping the omelet onto a plate when John walked into the room. "Something smells good."

"Would you like a Spanish omelet? It will only take me a few minutes to make you one." She considered offering him hers but couldn't bring herself to do it.

"Eat yours before it gets cold. I'll have coffee for now."

She was too hungry to argue with him. "I'm afraid I haven't made any. Coffee doesn't agree with me now. This is sad because I normally love coffee."

"Will it bother you if I make some?"

"Not at all."

"*Goot*, because I need a cup or four." He ran a hand through his hair, leaving it sticking up every which way.

Willa was tempted to smooth it for him but resisted the urge. "Did you figure out how to fix my grandfather's buggy?"

"I need to replace several large bolts that are missing from the frame and fifth wheel, the mechanism that allows the front wheels to turn in the same direction that the horse does. I wonder how my mother managed to get them off?"

Willa paused with her fork halfway to her mouth. "You don't really think your mother crawled under the buggy and loosened those bolts, do you? We could have been hurt if it had come apart while we were traveling. She wouldn't risk that."

"It wouldn't have rolled a foot the way it was. Someone knew what she was doing. I know Lucy and Megan couldn't have done it. That leaves my mother or you, and I'm willing to give you the benefit of the doubt considering your condition." He began spooning coffee grounds into the percolator.

"Couldn't they have simply worn out over time and fallen off yesterday? It is an old buggy. My grandfather never was one to invest in equipment upkeep. Is there any ketchup?"

He opened the refrigerator door, pulled out a bottle and handed it to her. "That possibility exists, but I didn't find any broken bolts on the ground. As I said, it wouldn't have rolled more than a few inches before coming apart. I drove it over beside the house myself after I fixed the loose rear wheel. It seems unlikely that my mother removed the bolts and hid the ones I keep in my shop, but I can't put it past her. She was adamant that you and the children stay longer."

"She has been very sweet to us. The girls have taken a great liking to her." Willa squeezed a liberal amount of ketchup onto her eggs.

"Is that good for the baby?"

"Is what good for the baby?" She forked a bite into her mouth and closed her eyes. Delicious. She cut herself another piece.

"That." He pointed to her plate. "The peppers and onions and all that ketchup."

She shrugged. "Plenty of babies are born in Spain, so I assume Spanish omelets are safe for pregnant women."

"There are some antacid tablets in the medicine cabinet if you need them later."

She sat up straight and burped. "Thanks. I may need them, but it tastes so good I can't stop."

"I don't see how you have any room left for food after the way you ate last night. I've never seen a woman eat so many biscuits. You had six after eating half a chicken."

Her mouth dropped open. "In case you haven't noticed, I'm eating for two!"

"Are you sure there aren't more? Like five or six?"

"That's an awful thing to say."

"What are you two quarreling about at this hour of the morning?" Vera asked as she came into the room.

John gestured toward Willa. "She's determined to eat us out of house and home. Lock the cellar and hide the key so she can't get to the canned produce."

Willa finished her eggs and pushed back from the table. "Do you have canned peaches? Oh, that sounds so good."

Vera chuckled. "I do, and John will fetch them for you."

He headed toward the cellar door. "Shall I bring up a dozen jars, or do you think you'll need more?"

"A dozen will do for a start," she said with a chuckle.

"I have some material in my sewing room that I want you to look over to see if you can use any of it," Vera said.

Willa was still smiling at John's teasing as she followed Vera down the hall. To her surprise, she saw several framed photographs on Vera's dresser as she glanced through the open door to Vera's bedroom. Stepping inside, Willa saw the photographs were all family portraits of parents with four children, three boys and one girl who looked to be the same age as her daughters.

"Those are my *Englisch* daughter, her husband and their children," Vera explained.

"Does your bishop allow photographs?" Willa had never heard of such a thing.

"As long as I don't keep them on public display, he allows it. My daughter's family lives on the West Coast and I seldom get to see them, but she makes sure that I get at least two family photographs each year."

"Your church group is very progressive. My grand-father's church would shun anyone who kept photo-graphs."

"I don't allow photographs to be taken of myself, but one of the girls at the local school is a talented artist. She has sketched likenesses of John and me. I plan to give them to my daughter. They are coming the week after Christmas and plan to stay for two weeks this year. I'm so excited to see them. It's been four years since I last saw all of them." Her smile faded and sadness filled her eyes. "Not since my oldest son's funeral."

"You lost a son? I'm sorry, I didn't know."

"No reason why you should."

"John told me about his wife last night and how she died."

Vera set the photograph back on the dresser. "Did he? That is a surprise. I knew you needed to stay with us for a reason."

Willa tipped her head to the side. "You didn't rig our buggy to break so we couldn't leave, did you?"

"What a silly question. I'd better get started on breakfast for everyone. Look through the material in the next room and let me know if you can use any of it. We will have to buy snow pants and boots for the children. Ana Bowman stocks a small selection in her gift store."

"I don't have any money to buy their clothing. I can't accept more charity when you have already given us so much."

"That is your *Englisch* pride speaking. Shame on you. An Amish woman is humble before the Lord and the world, and she accepts help without quibbling. The girls need warm clothing. We are commanded to care for widows and orphans by our faith. You shall have what you need. I don't want to hear another word about the cost. The day will come when you are able to help someone in return. Is that understood?"

Being humble was harder than Willa remembered, but she nodded.

"*Goot.* I think I have enough green worsted wool to make the girls overcoats and I know I have enough white organdy to make several *kapps* for you and the girls. If you are going to become Amish, you and your children must have more than one set of Amish clothes to wear. You will have to help me with some of the sewing. My hands ache something dreadful today."

Willa realized Vera hadn't answered her question about the buggy, but she didn't press the issue. After all, she and her girls were safe and being well cared for, at least until the storm was over. Soon they would have to move on, but not today.

Willa remembered John's teasing that morning and realized she was going to miss him as much as his mother when she did leave. Maybe more.

When had she come to like him so much?

Chapter Seven

"Johnjohn, will you play with me?"

John looked up from his magazine that afternoon to see Lucy standing in front of his chair staring at him. "I'm busy. Play with your sister."

He started reading again. He hadn't seen Willa or his mother for several hours, but he had been out plowing the lane after the wind had subsided. Nick Bradley would have had a hard time getting in to pick him up for the meeting even with his four-wheel-drive vehicle. Some of the drifts had been four feet deep, but Pete and Jake had no trouble breaking through them.

He glanced out the window. The winter landscape was brilliant and sparkling under a thick layer of pristine snow. The sky was clear and blue without a trace of clouds. The snowstorm had ended before dawn after blowing for two days. His mother and Willa had vanished into his mother's sewing room for much of that time. He had spent most of the gray daylight hours in his workshop and had accomplished a goodly amount of work. He had an hour to catch up on his reading before the fire department meeting this evening.

Lucy tapped his knee. "Read me a story, please," she said again with added emphasis on the *please*.

He chose the safest answer he could think of. "Go ask your mother."

"Mama is sleeping. Story, please."

Willa was sleeping. That was a good thing. She needed her rest. "Then go ask my mother."

Lucy gave an exasperated sigh.

Megan was lying on the oval rug in front of the sofa stacking wooden blocks. "She say ask you."

He hadn't seen anything in his blacksmithing journal he felt would interest a three-year-old. "Lucy, I don't have a storybook for you."

"No story?" Lucy stuck out her lower lip. Were tears next?

Please, not that. Maybe he didn't need a book. "I reckon I could tell you a story instead of reading one. Will that work, Lucy?"

"Okeydokey." She crawled onto his lap before he could think of a way to stop her.

She held out her hand to Megan. "Sissy, come listen to story."

Megan eyed him with distrust and shook her head.

John gave her the distance she seemed to need. "Megan can hear the story just fine where she is." Now all he had to do was think of one.

"See my new dress?" Lucy smoothed the vibrant blue material that matched her eyes. He hadn't noticed before, but Megan was wearing an identical new outfit, as well. Their old dresses had been oversize and a dull gray color.

"I see, and Megan has a new dress, too. You both look very nice and very plain."

It was true. Their hair was parted in the middle and held back with blue plastic clips that peeked from beneath their snowy-white *kapps*. Their *kapps*, which were the right size, and for once they were both wearing them. They were two very Amish-looking children.

Lucy folded her hands together and gazed up at him. "Once upon a time…"

She was persistent if nothing else. He chuckled. "Who is telling this story, you or me?"

"You. Once upon a time…"

He leaned back and looked at the ceiling. He'd never told a child a story before. Where did he start? Perhaps with something they would recognize.

"Once upon a time…" He paused to grin at Lucy. She smiled back.

"Once upon a time there were two little girls who came to visit an Amish farm. They were sisters. The Amish word for sister is *shveshtah*." It wouldn't hurt for them to start learning the language if their mother intended to raise them in the faith.

Lucy rolled the strange word around on her tongue. John smothered a smile. "The sisters came to the farm in a buggy pulled by a *gual*, a horse. The sisters decided to visit the animals in the barn. What animals do you think they saw?"

"A cat!" Lucy shouted.

"That's right. They saw a fluffy yellow *katz*. They wanted to pet her, but she ran away to chase mice. What else did the girls see?"

Megan crept closer and leaned on the arm of his chair. "A cow."

"They did, they saw a milk cow. Our word for milk cow is *milchkuh*."

"Baby cows, too," Lucy added.

"A calf, a *kalb*. In fact, the sisters saw two. The *kalbs* were twins just like the sisters. What is the Amish word for sister, Lucy?"

"Shveshtah," Megan answered.

"Da shveshtahs kumm to the farm in a buggy pulled by a *gaul*. On the farm they saw a *katz*, a *milchkuh* and *kalbs* in the barn. The cat ran away, but the cow stayed to eat hay. The sisters looked at each other and said 'We want hay for supper, too.'"

Lucy shook her head. "We don't want hay."

"What about you, Megan? Would you like hay for supper?" he asked, hoping to draw her out.

She almost smiled but quickly made her yucky face. "No!"

"Me, neither," he said. "I want apple pie and ice cream, and that is the end of our story about sisters visiting an Amish farm."

"Are you *kinder* ready for supper?" his mother asked from the kitchen door. Willa stood behind her, smiling softly at him. She, too, wore a new dress out of the same blue material with a black apron over it. Like her daughters, the color matched her lovely eyes. She looked rested and pleased with him.

Warmth filled his chest at the approval in her gaze.

Lucy slid off his lap and grabbed Megan's hand. "I hungry."

"Good. I hope Vera fixed enough hay to feed everyone," Willa said as she turned away.

The girls skidded to a halt in the doorway. His mother burst out laughing. "She is teasing you. We are having ham and potato soup, not hay. Go wash your hands and then come to the *dish*."

"*Dish* is the Amish word for table," Willa said. "Put your toys away in Vera's room and then wash up."

The children went down the hall. His mother turned to John. "I had no idea that you were such an entertaining storyteller."

"It's a newfound skill. One born of desperation. Save some soup for me. I'll eat later. Nick should be here any minute to pick me up for the meeting."

Willa placed glasses on the table. "Now that you have told the girls one story, you will have to tell them more. Once is never enough with my daughters. Fortunately for you, we will be on our way as soon as you get our buggy back together."

He realized he wasn't as happy about that as he should be. He would miss them when they were gone. "I will get the nuts and bolts I need from Luke Bowman's hardware on the way home tonight"

"But you won't be able to work on the buggy tomorrow, and Willa can't travel. Tomorrow is church Sunday. She's coming to the prayer meeting with us."

Willa tipped her head to the side. "I'm not sure the girls are ready for an Amish church service."

"They will learn our ways as all Amish children do, by the example of their parent."

Vera folded her arms over her chest. "If you truly wish to rejoin our faith, you must start somewhere."

"You are right, of course."

John could see Willa was worried about their behavior or perhaps something else. "They are sweet children and young enough that much will be forgiven them."

"It's only that I hate to expose them to so many strangers at once. I know they will be uncomfortable, especially Megan. I have always stressed stranger danger. Megan takes it to heart. Lucy has never met a stranger."

Maybe he could get to the bottom of the mystery about her fears. "Why are you so worried about strangers?"

Willa cast his mother a sharp look. "Didn't you tell him?"

Vera turned her attention to the pot on the stove. "I may have forgotten to mention it."

"You forgot to tell me what?" he asked, not certain he wanted to know. Willa had her gaze fixed on the floor. His mother began ladling soup into the bowls lined up on the counter. The tension in the air was as thick as smoke. Something wasn't right.

The tromping of heavy boots on the porch caught John's attention. The outside door opened and Sheriff Nick Bradley walked in. John was surprised to see him in uniform. He pulled his trooper's hat from his head. The bright gold star on the front glinted in the lamplight. "Evening, folks."

The world rocked under Willa's feet as she struggled to draw breath. It wasn't possible. How had the police found her here? Had John told them? Had Vera? She had to get to the girls. They had to get away. She took a step back, but Vera grabbed her arm with a painful grip, forcing her to stand still.

"Good evening, Nick. Have you time for a bowl of my potato soup before you and John head out to your meeting?" Vera's cordial tone cut though Willa's panic.

The tall man pulled his trooper's hat off his head. "I wish I did, Vera, but I've got another fella to pick up and these roads are slow going."

"Then don't let me keep you."

He gestured toward Willa with his hat. "I don't believe I've met your visitor."

"I'm sure you haven't. She is visiting us for the first time. *Frau* Lapp, this is Sheriff Bradley. He is a fair-minded fellow and a *goot* friend to the Amish."

He smiled. "It's nice to meet you, ma'am."

Willa couldn't speak. She simply nodded once. *Please, God, don't let the girls come out until he is gone.*

It seemed God wasn't listening, for she heard giggles and pounding feet in the hallway, but only Lucy came in. At the sight of a stranger she rushed to hide behind Willa. Willa prayed Lucy wouldn't speak. Her English would give them away for sure.

The sheriff grinned and squatted to Lucy's level. He asked her name in flawless *Deitsh*. Willa swallowed hard. John stepped between her and the sheriff as he pulled on his coat. "She is a shy one. She barely speaks to me. We should get going."

Standing upright, the sheriff settled his hat on his head. "It was nice meeting you, *Frau* Lapp. You've got a mighty cute *kinder.*"

"Danki." She barely managed to utter the word.

The sheriff touched the brim of his hat and followed John out the door.

Willa's knees began shaking so hard she could barely stand. Vera pulled her toward a chair. "It's all right now."

Willa dropped onto the seat. "What shall I do? What do I do now?" She grabbed Lucy by the shoulders. "Where is Megan?"

"Putting toys away," Lucy whispered and then started crying.

Megan came in and quickly put her arm around Lucy. "Don't cry."

"Bad man," Lucy said between sobs.

"Willa, you are frightening your little ones," Vera said in a stern tone.

Pulling her daughters close to comfort them, she said, "The man is gone. We're fine." Willa looked at Vera. "Did you know he was coming?"

"I did."

"Why didn't you warn me? We could've stayed in my room until he left."

"And then you would have been more afraid, if that is possible. He saw you, and he saw Lucy. What did he see? An Amish *frau* with a child."

"I could've given myself away."

"You did not. *Gott* was with you. Now let us have supper before the soup gets cold."

"I don't think I can eat." Willa's hands were still shaking.

"Nonsense. Think of the *boppli*. You both need nourishment."

"Do you really think we fooled him?" Willa stared at the door, expecting the sheriff to return at any moment.

"Of course we didn't fool him. That would be dishonest. He saw exactly what I see. He saw a friend of mine and her little girl. Tomorrow is church. You will worship as one of us. You will sing the hymns you learned as a child and have not forgotten. More people will meet *Frau* Lapp, a sad young widow with two small children. No one will see an *Englisch* woman pretending to be Amish…because she does not exist."

"I'm not sure I can do it."

"You can if you do it for the right reason. Seek and you shall find comfort listening to the preachers as they share the word of *Gott*. Salvation is yours if you accept *Gott*'s will. Then you will know peace. You are safe here."

Willa wanted to believe her, but she couldn't take her eyes off the door.

John sat stiffly in the front seat of Nick's SUV. He didn't know what Willa was afraid of, but he would find out before this night was over. He'd seen the fear in her eyes when the sheriff came in. Her fingers had been clenched so tightly her knuckles stood out white against the blue of her dress.

Nick hadn't spoken since they got in the SUV. He turned into the lane of Stroud's horse farm. Noah Bowman, a neighbor and another Amish volunteer firefighter, lived on the stable grounds with his new wife. Nick stopped the car in front of their house and turned in his seat to face John. "*Frau* Lapp seemed upset to see me. Know any reason why she should be afraid of me?"

John expected his question. Nick was too good at his job not to have noticed Willa's reaction. John was glad he didn't know what was wrong. He shared what he knew to be the truth. "Her husband was recently killed in an automobile accident. The police brought her the bad news. I didn't think to tell her that an officer of the law was coming to the house tonight. Perhaps she feared more tragic news when she saw you."

"That explains a lot. Thank you. Please give her my condolences when you speak to her again and tell her I didn't mean to frighten her or dredge up bad memories."

"I will."

Nick started to open the car door, but Noah had seen them and hurried out of the house. He slid into the back seat. "*Guten nacht*, John. Evening, Nick. I appreciate the lift. What's new in the big bad world of law enforcement?"

"Same old thing. Drunk drivers, drug busts, drag racing, buggy racing, two missing-person reports. Oh, there was a report of a rabid squirrel trying to get in someone's front door last week. Turned out to be a pet that belonged to the man in the next apartment."

"Who has gone missing? Some of our Amish kids?" Noah asked.

It was sad, but some youth who didn't wish to join the faith felt so pressured to do so that they saw running away in the dead of night as their only way out.

Nick turned the SUV around. "One was a boy from Bishop Troyer's church. Your brother Luke still runs a counseling group for kids who want to leave, doesn't he? Ask him if he knows anything about the boy."

"I will, but you know Luke deeply respects the privacy of those who come to him."

"I appreciate that. The number of runaways in this area has gone down 50 percent since he started his group. The other missing people aren't Amish. It's a woman from Columbus with three-year-old twin daughters. They were last seen getting off a bus outside of Millersburg, and then they vanished into thin air."

"That doesn't sound good," Noah said.

Nick shook his head. "We don't suspect foul play. According to the Columbus police, the woman is involved in a custody situation. They think she disappeared on purpose."

"Millersburg is quite a ways from here," John said. "Any reason to think she is in our area?"

"None, but we're conducting a statewide search. We take missing children seriously. I wish we had posters to put up, but strangely there aren't any photographs of this woman or her children."

"They must be Amish," Noah joked.

Nick chuckled. "They aren't Amish. Her husband was wanted for embezzlement before he was killed about six months ago. She's about five feet two inches tall with blond hair and blue eyes. The twins are blonde with blue eyes, too. The woman was last seen wearing a red coat and carrying a purple backpack. That's all we know."

Noah leaned forward. "Is she a criminal, too?"

"Let's just say we want to talk to her."

John remained silent. Nick had just described Willa the first day they met. No wonder she looked frightened when Nick came through the front door. Why were they looking for her and her children? What had she done? He was tempted to ask Nick but decided he owed Willa the chance to explain.

The men arrived at the fire station a short time later. John put his concerns about Willa aside and concentrated on the meeting he was required to attend. The safety of his community and his fellow firefighters might depend on the information that was shared by the emergency preparedness officers. It wasn't until they were on their way to Noah's later that evening that John wondered exactly how he was going to question Willa.

Nick's cell phone rang as he turned into the horse farm. He pulled it from his pocket and listened to the caller for a minute before he said, "I'm heading home now. I'll pick up Joshua and Mary. We'll meet you at the hospital in thirty minutes."

He hung up. Noah leaned forward in the back seat. "Is something wrong?"

"My wife thinks her mother is having another heart attack. It doesn't look good."

Noah laid a hand on Nick's shoulder. "Let us know if we can help."

"I will. I need to get going."

Nick drove John home and then took off with his red lights flashing as soon as John was out of the car. John climbed the steps slowly and opened his front door with reluctance.

Willa was waiting at the kitchen table when John walked in. Her face was pale, but she looked composed. She clutched a mug of coffee in her hands. Before he could speak, she said, "I have some explaining to do, but would you like your supper first?"

"Our fire chief brought pizza for everyone, so you don't need to fix me anything."

She took a deep breath and raised her chin. "That's too bad. I was hoping for a short reprieve. What did Sheriff Bradley say about me?"

"He noticed that you were frightened, and he asked me if I knew why."

She pressed her lips tightly together. "What did you tell him?"

"Only what I know, which isn't much. I told him that your husband died recently, that a police officer brought you the news and that you weren't expecting to see another officer at our door tonight. He also mentioned there is a missing-person report for a woman with twin daughters who got off a bus outside Millersburg."

Willa rubbed her hands up and down her arms as if she were cold. "I can't believe they tracked me to the bus station so quickly."

He took a seat opposite her at the table. "Willa, who is looking for you?"

She gripped her mug again and lifted her chin to meet his gaze. "My husband's parents are looking for me. They want custody of my daughters. They want to raise them as their own and to make sure I never see them."

He didn't understand. "How would such a thing be possible? Have they told you this?"

"I have never met them, but that is what they told Glen. My husband said they filed a police report claiming we were unfit parents a month after the girls were born and that a judge had granted them temporary custody. Glen said we could never fight them in court. They have too much money and too much influence, so we took the babies and ran. If his parents or the police locate us, they will take the girls away from me and I may never see them again. I could even go to jail for disobeying a court order."

John read the sincerity in Willa's frank gaze. He raked a hand through his hair. He didn't know what he had been expecting, but it wasn't this.

She took a sip of her coffee and waited for him to speak. He had no idea what to say. He couldn't imagine his friend Nick taking the twins away from their mother. "Your husband's parents have been looking for you since the girls were newborns?"

"They have a private investigator looking for us. My husband spent the last three years trying to keep our whereabouts a secret, but we were always discovered. Many times we had to leave at a moment's notice to avoid being caught."

"That must have been a difficult way to live."

She lowered her gaze. "It was. It took money and planning to hide from those looking for us. Glen was the one who did all that. I simply followed him. I discovered how difficult it was after he was gone. I couldn't do it alone."

"Why go to your grandfather? Surely his family would know to look for you among your relatives."

"Glen told them I was an orphan when he called them to tell them he had gotten married. He thought they would stop hounding him if he proved he was starting a new life. As far as I know, Glen's family has no idea I was raised Amish. He was ashamed of my backward ways, my odd speech, my ignorance of modern technology. I tried very hard to become English enough for him."

John could tell by the sadness in her eyes that she hadn't been able to accomplish her mission. "So you came to hide among us."

"I didn't know what else to do. I prayed my family would take us in. My grandfather wouldn't. He didn't believe I sincerely wanted to return to the faith, but he told me to go to his sister in Hope Springs. He loaned me the horse and buggy for the trip. You know the rest of the story."

"Your plan is still to continue to Hope Springs?"

"It is. I'm hoping and praying that no one will look for me there. I love my daughters more than my own life. I will do anything to keep them with me. The question now is what will you do with this information?"

John hadn't known Willa long, but she wasn't an unfit mother. He was certain of that. "Nick Bradley is a friend, but he is an outsider. The *Englisch* ways are not our ways. We have our own laws laid down by God and the church. The law that says you are a poor mother is an unjust law."

She breathed a deep sigh of relief. "It means a lot to hear you say that."

"I'm pleased you feel you can confide in me."

A pink flush stained her cheeks. "You and your mother deserve to know the truth."

He rose to his feet and crossed to the sink, not wanting her to see how moved he was by her trust in him. After years of hiding and then finding out he was friends with the sheriff, it had taken courage for her to reveal her story. He poured out his cold coffee.

Willa brought her cup to empty it into the sink, too. "Do you think the sheriff will come back? That he will guess who I am?"

"He said he isn't looking for an Amish woman. He has met you and he has no reason to doubt you are anything but a visiting Amish friend of ours."

They stood shoulder to shoulder in the silence of the still house. He looked down at her bowed head. The top of her *kapp* wouldn't reach his chin unless she stood on tiptoe. She was such a tiny woman to bear such a large burden. It would be easy to put his arm around her and draw her close.

The thought shocked him. He never imagined he would want another woman in his arms after Katie died, but he did. He wanted to hold Willa and not just to comfort her. He wanted to be comforted by her. The urge was overwhelming. He had to grip the edge of the sink to keep his hands from doing just that.

He had no right to touch her and no reason to think she would welcome his embrace. "You are a brave woman, Willa Lapp. I've never met anyone quite like you."

"I don't feel brave." She slanted a glance up at him. "Will you tell your bishop about me?"

"Since you are leaving, I don't see the need to inform him about this, but I urge you to do so when you reach your family in Hope Springs. It is always wise to seek the council of holy men."

"I'm sorry I put you in a difficult position with your friend. It is a poor way to repay your kindness. I did tell your mother all of this. I assumed that she would tell you."

"It makes me wonder why she did not."

"You don't think it simply slipped her mind?"

He gave her a wry smile and shook his head. "Not for a minute."

Chapter Eight

The sound of tires crunching through the snow outside brought Willa bolt upright in bed later that night. Car lights shone through the window. Had the sheriff come back? Was he going to take her children?

She jumped out of bed, pulled a robe over her night-gown and rushed into the hall. John came out of his room fully dressed. He carried a flashlight in his hand. The beam illuminated a circle on the floor, but it gave enough light for her to see his face. "It's all right, Willa. Go back to bed. I'm being called out for a fire."

The painful hammering of her heart slowed. "I thought the sheriff had returned."

"It is only the *Englisch* neighbor who collects Amish volunteers in our area." He spoke softly.

As her panic receded, she realized he was heading out to fight a blaze in frigid conditions. Would it be dangerous for him? "What kind of fire is it?"

He stood inches away from her. "I don't know the details. I'll learn more when I reach the fire station."

"Be careful, John."

He touched her cheek. "I trust God to keep me safe as you should, too."

She wanted to grasp his hand, but she didn't. "I sometimes think He is busy elsewhere and isn't paying attention to me."

"Never think that. He is with us always. Go back to bed." He slipped past her and went out the door, letting in a blast of cold air.

She pulled her robe more tightly around her. She hadn't realized how much she did doubt God's mercy until this instant. The faith that had sustained her since childhood hung by a thread. What kind of life would she have if she lost it?

Unable to go back to bed, she went into the kitchen and made a sandwich for herself and one for John in case he was hungry when he returned. Spreading the mayo, she realized she hadn't given a thought to the people affected by the fire. Laying down her knife, she folded her hands and asked God to watch over John and the other firefighters. The lives or livelihoods of a family somewhere might be in peril. She prayed for them, too.

Picking up her knife again, she finished cutting the sandwich and carried her plate into the living room, where the window looked out toward the lane. She settled in a chair, ate a few bites and kept watch for John's return.

The clouds in the east held the barest hint of pink when a red pickup turned into the lane and stopped by the house. John got out, and the vehicle drove away. She couldn't help but notice the tired slump of his shoulders as he approached the house.

He looked surprised when she opened the door for him. "What are you doing up so early?"

Willa stretched her stiff neck as she took in his grime-covered face. "I couldn't sleep. You look tired. Was it a bad fire?"

"Bad enough." He walked into the kitchen, turned on the water and began to wash his face.

She waited until he finished washing and drying off. "Was it a family you know?"

He shook his head. "A gasoline tanker truck missed a corner and overturned on the highway about four miles south of here. The truck caught on fire. We managed to get the driver out before the truck exploded. It was a near thing. Then we had to keep the fire from spreading to a nearby house. We did with the help of another fire crew. The driver had some injuries, but the paramedics said they thought he'd be okay."

"That is a wonderful blessing."

"Some family will have a much happier Christmas, that's for sure."

"I made you a sandwich, but would you like me to cook something?"

"A sandwich is fine. I'm going to try to catch a few winks before we have to leave for church. You should do the same."

"I will."

She started down the hallway but stopped when he spoke. "Thanks for waiting up for me."

"I knew I was going to worry, so there was no point in trying to sleep."

"To worry is to doubt God."

"Perhaps, but it's a skill I have perfected." She walked on down the hall and wondered if that would ever change.

* * *

John woke when the sunlight brightened his room. A glance at the clock showed it was time to get his chores done before church. He swung his legs over the side of the bed and sat up. Had Willa gotten any sleep? She needed to take better care of herself.

He dressed quickly in the cold room. As he started to make the bed, he realized he hadn't thought about Katie for almost an entire day. Missing her beside him had been his first thought each morning and his last thought at night since her death. This morning his first thoughts had been for Willa.

He sat on the side of the bed and waited for the sharp pain of grief to return, but it didn't. He missed Katie. He missed her friendship and her smile, but he remembered those things with a gentle sadness. What had changed? He knew the answer as soon as the question formed in his mind.

Willa and her daughters had brought a new energy into his home, and if he admitted the truth, she brought a special light into his life. He saw himself more clearly. He saw how crippling his grief had been. He would always miss Katie, but perhaps it was time to lay his sorrow to rest.

An hour later John stomped the snow from his boots on the front porch and stepped onto the rag rug inside the kitchen. Willa was wiping strawberry jelly from Lucy's face. He noticed the dark circles under her eyes had reappeared. She had been too worried about him to sleep. Did that mean she cared about him?

Today was her last day with them. A few days ago, he had been eager to see the last of her. Now he didn't want to think about her leaving. When had he become such a fickle fellow?

He knew the answer. When Willa had slipped her hand in his and said that she trusted him. He wasn't sure he had earned her trust, but it pleased him to know she gave it freely.

"We're almost ready." She turned to wipe Megan's face next and lifted her from the booster seat his mother had unearthed from somewhere.

"Bundle them up well. It'll be a cold ride. Are you sure you are up for this?"

She straightened and pressed a hand to the small of her back. "Ask me in an hour. Can we make it through this much snow with the buggy?"

"The roads have been plowed. We won't have any trouble. You may want to put some bricks in your pockets today as long as they are hot ones. You'll need them."

She gave him a sad smile. "At least you won't have to try to lift me up onto the wagon the way you did a little over a week ago."

Was that all it had been since he'd met her on the road to her grandfather's farm? Sometimes he forgot she was little more than a stranger. It felt as if he had known her for ages.

She grimaced and bent from side to side. "My aching back is not looking forward to the drive. I didn't have this kind of pain during my pregnancy with the girls until I went into labor."

He reeled with shock. "Are you in labor now? Shall I get the midwife? Where is my mother?"

She had the nerve to laugh at him. "I'm not in labor, John. I know what that feels like. This feels like I've been lifting twenty-pound sacks of potatoes all morning."

He strode past her to lift Lucy out of her high chair, hoping to hide the red tide he felt rising up his neck. "Perhaps too many *rundlich boppli* like this one."

Willa took Lucy from him and balanced the girl on her hip. "She is not a plump baby. She is exactly where she should be for her age." She scowled at his feet. "And you are getting my clean floor dirty."

He looked at the trail of melting snow and barn muck he'd left as he crossed the kitchen. "It is my floor. I will get it dirty if it pleases me."

Her eyebrows shot up. "I hope it pleases you to mop it. I've already done that once this morning, and I need to get the children ready for church. The mop is on the back porch." She tipped her head toward the door and walked out of the room.

John allowed a smile to slip free as he watched her carry Lucy to the back bedroom. Megan followed after her.

"What are you grinning about?" his mother asked as she came in from the living room. She carried several flannel-wrapped bricks that she placed in the oven.

"Willa is sadly lacking in *demut*. Have you noticed that?"

"*Nee*, I have not noticed a lack of the humbleness in her, but why should that make you smile?"

"Because it is my kitchen floor."

"You aren't making any sense. Are you sick?" She reached up to lay a hand on his forehead.

"*Nee*, I'm not sick. Make sure Willa and the girls are bundled well and you do the same. I don't want you coming down sick."

"Don't worry about me. I feel fine." She glanced toward the back bedroom. "It is our last day together. I will miss them when they go. This house hasn't felt so alive in years."

"*Kinder* have a way of doing that," he said softly. Having the twins and their mother around had been as disruptive as he'd feared, but he was growing used to them.

"I wonder what frightens her so much," his mother said softly.

He frowned. "I thought she was afraid her husband's parents will take her children away."

"There is that, but she is safe with us and she knows it. I feel something else has her deeply worried. I wish she would confide in us."

His mother enjoyed gossip, as much if not more than the next person did, but she wasn't given to imagining things. If she believed Willa was afraid of something else, she probably was.

Turning to face him, his mother laid a hand on his chest. "John, will you drive Willa to Hope Springs when the weather clears? I don't want her traveling there by herself. I hate to think of her out on the roads alone in the winter. Her horse could slip and fall. Anything could happen."

He had been thinking the same thing. "I have a sleigh to finish. I can't take four days away from my work to drive to Hope Springs and back."

It was a poor excuse and he knew it.

"Please, son, for my peace of mind."

He didn't want to endure a lingering goodbye. A quick break was the best. "I'll arrange for a driver to ke her there in a comfortable car. Will that make you el better?"

His mother frowned. "I thought we couldn't afford to hire a driver."

He couldn't afford it, but with the money he had been promised for his work on the vis-à-vis, he could pay part of it and perhaps barter for the rest with one of the local drivers. "I'll work something out. Willa will be much more comfortable and can make the trip in a few hours."

"If you think that is best, I agree. We're going to be late for church if I don't hurry up and get ready. The food hamper is packed. Will you take it out for me?" She started down the hallway to her room, but she didn't look or sound pleased.

"I will as soon as I finish mopping the floor," he called after her.

She stopped and turned back. "What did you say?"

"Never mind. Don't forget to bring the bricks."

She gave a slight shake of her head and walked into her room. John mopped his way backward from the door to the counter where the hamper sat and then out the kitchen door. He left the mop leaning against the porch railing.

After placing the hamper on the back seat, he walked up to stand beside Clover and scratched the mare under her chin. "This should be an interesting church service. I am guessing that Lucy and Megan will have a hard time sitting still on our wooden benches. Let's pray the bishop and the preachers give short sermons today."

Vera was already in the back seat of the buggy when Willa finally made it out the door with both the girls dressed in their new Sunday clothing. It had been a fight to keep Megan's bonnet on her head and Lucy's shoes on her feet, but they looked sweet and very Ami in their deep purple, ankle-length dresses and *eahmal shatzli*, the long white aprons worn by little girls. Willa was especially pleased with their forest green woolen coats. She and Vera had worked hard to get them finished in time. Both girls wore black traveling bonnets over their *kapps* to keep their heads warm on the ride. She and Vera wore bonnets, too.

John stood patiently beside the horse. He looked quite handsome in his black Sunday suit and his flat-topped, wide-brimmed black hat.

Willa mentally corrected herself. He looked very plain. His eyes brightened as he met her gaze. If only she could find a way to still the flutter in her midsection when he smiled at her. His kindnesses the previous evening made her respect and admire him even more. It was a good thing that she was leaving tomorrow, because she was becoming very fond of him. Too fond.

"I'm sorry if I have made us late." She hoped he attributed her breathless tone to battling with her daughters.

"I know who to blame for your tardiness." He leveled a stern look at her girls. "The next time you disobey your *mamm*, you will have extra chores to do."

"We'll be good," Lucy said, her eyes round as saucers.

"And you, Megan? Will you do what your mother tells you?"

She nodded. "Hat's on. See?" She smoothed the sides of her bonnet.

He crouched down to their level and smiled at them. "*Goot*. When you honor your mother, you please God and that pleases me."

"Okeydokey." Lucy patted his cheek.

He lifted the girls into the back seat with his mother. She already had the hot bricks on the floor to warm their feet and spread a quilt over their legs. Willa looked in and frowned slightly. "Don't you want to ride up front, Vera?"

"I'm fine here with the girls to keep me warm. It's best that you sit up front. Sitting in the back when I was pregnant always made me queasy. I don't want you feeling sick during the service."

In that instant Willa realized John's mother was trying to foster a romance between the two of them. The elderly woman was going to be sadly disappointed if she hoped to sway Willa from leaving. She might have gotten away with loosening the wheels of Willa's buggy, but she wasn't going to be able to pull the same stunt again. The very idea of his mother's meddling would have been funny if not for the fact that Willa already liked John far too much. She liked Vera, too, and the girls adored her, but a relationship with John wasn't possible.

Willa had to leave. She had to have her family around her when her baby was born.

John took hold of Willa's elbow to steady her as she climbed in the buggy. Willa smiled her thanks, but she wasn't smiling inside. Love and marriage were out of the question for her no matter how much she might wish it could be otherwise.

He tucked the thick lap robe around her. "Are you warm enough?"

"I'm fine." She looked away from the concern in his eyes. He climbed into the front seat and slapped the reins to get the horse moving.

They arrived at the home of Hank Hochstetler and his family about forty minutes later. They weren't late. The service hadn't started, but they were the last to arrive. Vera got out with Willa and the girls as John parked his buggy among the two dozen other vehicles that lined the lane and unhitched his horse.

Vera took Willa's arm. "Be careful on this ice. Hank runs a small engine repair business. The service will be held in his shop. His home is too small to accommodate all of us."

Willa entered the metal building and almost backed out when she saw the number of people inside. She closed her eyes and drew a deep breath. As nervous as she was, she knew she couldn't let it show. The twins clutched her coat and looked at her in concern.

"It's okay," she whispered to them.

Vera took them both by the hand. "There are only friends here, so there is nothing to be scared of."

"Let's sit near the back in case I need to take the girls out," Willa said, knowing it was unlikely her girls could remain quiet for three or more hours of preaching in *Dietsh* with Bible readings in High German. Amish children were expected to mirror their parents and elders with a somber devout demeanor during the service, but exceptions were made for children as young as the twins.

Willa followed Vera into the building and felt the weight of all the eyes watching her. A new person at church was always a cause for curiosity.

The inside of the workshop was spotlessly clean. She knew the family and friends of the owner would have spent days making sure every surface was cleaned inside and out. The workload for hosting a service was such that each family in the congregation was expected to host only once a year.

The backless wooden benches were lined up either

side of the center aisle. Men and boys sat on one side while women and girls sat on the other side. Around the perimeter, a few padded chairs had been carried out from the house for some of the more elderly members. The room was a sea of black on the men's side. Black coats and pants were the standard Sunday dress code. Identical black hats hung from a long row of pegs on the back wall.

The women were more colorful. Their long dresses and matching aprons were an assortment of solid colors, blue, green and mauve. Vera took her place on one of the benches and patted the seat beside her, indicating the girls should sit next to her.

From the men's side, the *volsinger*, the hymn leader, began the first song. He had a fine, steady voice. After the first line, the rest of the congregation joined in. The slow and mournful chanting reverberated inside the steel building as members blended their voices together without musical accompaniment. The opening song, like all Amish hymns, had been passed down through the generations for more than seven hundred years. Willa picked up the heavy black songbook, the *Ausbund*. It contained the words of the song but no musical notations. Every song in the book has been learned and remembered by members of the faith down through the ages.

The second song of an Amish church service was always the same hymn. *"Das Loblied,"* a song of love and praise. Willa was astonished at how easily the words and melody came back to her. It was as if she had last sung it yesterday instead of ten years ago.

She had kept God in her heart, but there was something special about worshipping with others. The bishop was an eloquent speaker who filled his sermon with praise for God, his great works and his unending mercy. His heartfelt words sparked a ray of new hope in Willa. Vera had been right. Willa drew deep comfort from the preaching and the songs. She didn't have to be alone. She could become part of a larger community bound together by faith and a commitment to each other.

This prayer meeting was the first step in her journey back to that faith. Not to hide among the Amish, but to become one of them again if God so willed it.

She prayed fervently that it was His will. That her family would welcome her and that the sheriff would never discover her real identity.

Chapter Nine

Twice during the service Willa took the girls out when they became restless. Once when Lucy needed to use the bathroom and again a half an hour later when Megan decided she needed to go.

Willa walked the girls up to the house and saw she wasn't the only mother missing part of the preaching. A tall woman with unusual violet-blue eyes and blond hair was changing a fussy baby in the bedroom across from the bathroom.

"Mama, baby cry," Megan whispered. A worried look filled her eyes.

"He will be fine in a minute," the mother said as she finished wrapping her son in a blanket before lifting him to her shoulder. As promised, he quieted immediately.

Willa sent Megan into the bathroom and waited outside with Lucy.

The woman walked toward Willa, her eyes sparkling as she smiled at Lucy. "I have two, but they are a year apart. I'm not sure I could manage twins. How old are your girls?"

"They turned three last month. How old is your son?"

"Two months. I'm Rebecca Bowman, and this is Henry."

"I'm Willa Lapp, and this is Lucy. Her sister is Megan."

"I was surprised to hear such a little one speaking English. You aren't from this area, are you? Do you have family here?"

Willa had known this would happen. With so many people around, someone was bound to overhear the girls speaking English. She gave a carefully edited version of her circumstances. "My husband wasn't Amish. He only wanted the girls to speak English, so I never taught them *Deitsh*. He passed away a few months ago, and I returned to my Amish family. The girls and I were on our way to visit my great-aunt, but my buggy broke down near John Miller's place. He and his mother took us in during the storm."

"Vera and John are *goot* people. I know them well. I was married to Vera's oldest son. Like you, I became a widow at a young age, but God smiled on me and now I have a new *wunderbar* husband and two busy boys." She kissed the head of her infant. "When is your baby due?"

"The second week in January." Willa pulled her coat closed. She had hoped to keep her pregnancy a secret, but Rebecca had sharp eyes.

"That makes you about thirty-three weeks along?"

"Almost."

"I remember how much I wanted those last weeks of pregnancy to fly by. I felt like a fat waddling goose by the end."

The fear of a relapse left Willa wishing she could stay pregnant forever. "I'm not in a hurry. I have so much to do first."

"If only they would listen to our wishes, but babies often show up at the most inconvenient times. If your family is in the area, Janice Willard is an excellent nurse-midwife. She isn't Amish, but she could be. I can give you her phone number."

"My family lives several days from here and I will be leaving tomorrow, but thank you."

"I washed my hands," Megan said, coming out of the bathroom and holding her palms up for Willa to inspect.

"That's very good."

"Goot," Megan said. She gazed up at Rebecca. "Can I see baby?"

"They will pick up our language quick enough." Rebecca smiled and dropped to one knee. She opened the blanket so Megan could gaze at the baby's face.

"I like baby," Megan said softly.

Rebecca looked up at Willa. "That bodes well for your new addition."

"It does. I hope it is a boy."

Rebecca rose and spoke to Megan. "Henry has a brother named Benjamin. You can meet him after church is over."

Willa took both her daughters by the hand. "We should get back to the service."

"No, me tired." Lucy pulled away and stuck out her lip.

Rebecca chuckled. "I feel the same way. It won't last much longer, and then you can get something *goot* to eat. Do you know what church spread is?"

Lucy brightened instantly. "Yes, yummy."

"I think it's yummy, too." Rebecca winked as Willa held her hand out to Lucy. "Let's go see if the bishop is done talking."

"Okeydokey." Lucy smiled brightly at her new friend.

The bishop was finished, but another of the preachers was just getting started when they returned to their seats. All in all, Willa was pleased with how well her daughters behaved. They conducted themselves much better than the young boy of about three who roamed back and forth between his parents, going the long way around the room each time at a run. From the looks cast his way by several of the elders, Willa suspected the boy's father would hear from them after the meeting.

Following the church service, Vera walked beside Willa to the house, where the meal would be held. "I didn't see Mary, Joshua or Ana Bowman in church. They must be visiting somewhere. I wanted you to meet Mary and find out if she knows your family in Hope Springs."

"I met Rebecca Bowman a little while ago."

"Did she tell you she was once my daughter-in-law?"

"She did."

"She is a fine woman. I had hoped that she and John would make a match of it, but *Gott* had different plans for them. Come, I want you to meet some friends of mine."

Inside, the house was a beehive of activity as women unpacked hampers and arranged food on the counters. Vera introduced Willa to many of the married women and a few of the single women in the congregation. It surprised Willa how friendly the women all seemed.

The benches were quickly carried in and restacked to form tables and seating for the meal. Since there wasn't enough room to feed everyone at once, the ordained and eldest church members ate first. The youngest among the congregation would have to wait until last. Few of the youngsters seemed to mind, for they were all busy playing with their friends.

Rebecca won Megan's heart when she had the girl sit in a chair and hold Henry for a little while. Lucy wasn't interested in the baby, but she did watch some of the other children closely. Willa could tell she wanted to play with them, but she wasn't willing to leave her sister. When Rebecca took Henry back, the twins were drawn away by a pair of school-aged girls who had been charged with looking after the younger children while the women prepared and served the noon meal.

Willa began unpacking the hamper of food the Millers had provided. There was bread, cold cuts, pickles and homemade pretzels along with the traditional church spread of peanut butter and marshmallow cream. Other women unpacked cheeses, pies, cookies and assorted baked goods. It was far different Sunday fare than had been served in the Swartzentruber group where Willa grew up. She recalled everyone eating bean soup from a common bowl along with bread, beets and pickles.

She heard her girls laughing and looked up to see them enjoying a game of tag with the other children. A pang of regret hit her hard. She pressed a hand to her mouth.

"What's wrong?" Vera asked.

Willa didn't realize she was being watched so closely. "Glen and I never stayed in one place long enough for the girls to make friends. It's nice to see them having fun with children their own age. I wish he were here to see it."

"Your *kinder* will have many chances to make friends when you settle into a new community. Is your heart set on going to Hope Springs? You could always remain here. You would be most welcome."

The idea would be tempting if she weren't afraid of her illness returning. "My heart is set on getting to know my family again."

"Of course. Still, it is something to consider after your reunion with your relatives. You might not like them."

Willa laughed out loud. "If they are anything like you, I will love them. I can always return to visit you."

"You must promise to do so. I've grown fond of you. John has, too, although he doesn't like to show it."

Willa's grin faded and she looked away. "John is a kind man."

"Is he the kind of man you might consider as a husband?" she asked hopefully.

Willa quickly shook her head. John would make a fine husband, but not for her. Marriage would mean more children and more chances to hurt them. "I won't marry again."

"You are too young to say this. Forgive the meddling of an old woman who would like to see her son happy again."

Willa managed a half-hearted smile. "You are forgiven. What can I do now?"

Rebecca appeared at her elbow. "You can help me set the tables."

"I can do that." Willa jumped at the chance to escape Vera's watchful eyes. If only she could escape the sudden longing Vera's suggestion had unleashed in her heart.

Willa followed Rebecca's lead and began setting a knife, fork, cup and saucer at each place. Vera came along behind them pouring coffee into the cups. Some of the women were rolling up their sleeves, ready to wash the plates and cups as soon as the diners were done with them; others were cutting cakes and desserts. Everyone was chatting and laughing.

Willa was amazed at how natural it felt to be doing such ordinary tasks with Vera and her friends. For a little while, she forgot about being discovered or needing to constantly look over her shoulder. Everyone accepted her at face value. Much of the talk among the women was about the fire the previous night and how thankful they were that it hadn't been worse. A few talked about visiting family for Thanksgiving, but the conversation soon turned to Christmas and everyone's plans.

Lillian Bowman, one of the teachers, announced the school program would be held twice this year because of the number of people expected to attend. The children would perform at two o'clock and again at six o'clock on Christmas Eve. Willa's school Christmas programs had been some of the highlights of her childhood, as they were for all Amish children. She thought of her girls and knew she wanted them to experience the same excitement over the true meaning of Christmas as she had when she was young.

Returning to join the Amish might have been an act of desperation on her part, but Willa began to believe it was also the best decision. She had been one week away from making that choice when she was fifteen. So much had changed in the intervening years, but now that she was twenty-five, she was free to make her choice again.

Rebecca and her sister-in-law Fannie Bowman told the women they had plans to take several groups caroling on December 19. Everyone who wanted to join them could meet at the Stroud Stables at three o'clock. The bishop's wife called for everyone's attention and said she planned to hold a cookie exchange on the twenty-third as long as she could keep the bishop from eating all the cookies until everyone arrived.

Willa was laughing with the others when she looked across the room and met John's gaze. He had come in to eat. He gave her a small smile and a nod. She felt the color rush to her cheeks, but she smiled back.

Looking down, she laid another knife by a cup and saucer. She could almost pretend this was her family and her church group and that this was where she belonged. That the plans for Christmas included her and her children. When she looked up again, John stood across the table from her. He said, "It's nice to see you looking happy among us."

She glanced toward the women gathered in the kitchen. "I have missed this feeling of belonging and sharing. I didn't realize how much until today."

"I pray you find it again where you are going."

It seemed as if he wanted to say more, but he didn't. He took his plate to the table and left shortly afterward.

Had John come to care for her as his mother had suggested. She was flattered, but she hoped his mother was mistaken. Willa didn't want to hurt his feelings. He had suffered so much loss in his life already. She didn't want to add to his sadness.

Willa looked for him outside after she had eaten lunch and helped the women clean up. She scanned the farmyard and quickly located him. He was easy to pick out in the sea of black suits and hats for he stood a good head taller than most of the men standing outside in the cold sunshine. He was joking and smiling as he visited with them. The mood in this community was so much brighter and happier than the church group where she had grown up. Wouldn't it be wonderful if her great-aunt's congregation were like this one?

A group of teenage girls passed Willa on their way to the large shed now empty of benches. There would be volleyball and other games held inside the spacious building. Most of the youths in their *rumspringa* would remain for the singing that would be held after supper that evening. After that, many would pair up for a buggy or sleigh ride home with a date. Willa had looked forward eagerly to her *rumspringa*, her running around time, when she was growing up, but her father's decision to leave the faith had prevented her from having a normal Amish teenage life. How different would her life have been if he hadn't made that choice?

She didn't blame him. He had his reasons for leaving. Willa's mother had suffered from deep bouts of depression, something the community and others in the family didn't understand. His attempts to get her help from outside had been met with firm disapproval. Her father left to get her mother the help she needed, but in the end, it didn't matter. Her mother accidently took too many of the pills Willa's father was sure would help. Willa knew he simply gave up on life after his wife's death. They were both gone before Willa turned nineteen. If not for meeting Glen, Willa had no idea what she would have done. He became her rock. In spite of the sorrow that had touched her life, Willa knew she was blessed. She wouldn't have Lucy and Megan if she hadn't married Glen. She wouldn't trade being their mother for anything.

John noticed her and nodded in her direction. She

gestured to the empty hamper she carried and then to the buggy so he knew what she was doing.

She was looking about for the twins when John approached with an older man he introduced as Isaac Bowman. "Isaac has some news about his daughter-in-law Mary."

Willa brightened. "I looked forward to meeting her today. I understand she is from Hope Springs. I have family in that area that I haven't seen in many years. I was hoping she might know them."

"Mary, my son Joshua and my wife left here late last night to go to the hospital in Millersburg. We had received word that Mary's grandmother had fallen ill. She used to live with Joshua and Mary, but she moved in with her daughter in Hope Springs last fall. I learned a short time ago that she passed away. Our family will be leaving to attend the funeral in Hope Springs later this week. I'm sure Mary will be happy to visit with you about the folks she knows when she returns."

Willa hid her disappointment. "I'm sorry for her loss. I'm leaving tomorrow, so I won't have the chance to meet her."

Vera came to join them beside the sleigh. "I just heard about Ada. What a shame. I know how much she loved Mary and how she adored little Hannah. Many people will miss her. Do we know what happened?"

"Only that she passed away," Isaac said.

Vera shook her head. "It's so sad, but Ada Kaufman lived a long life. We grieve for you and your family, but we also rejoice in the knowledge that she is with our Lord in heaven."

Willa's breath caught in her throat. Ada Kaufman was her great-aunt's name. They couldn't be talking about her, could they? Surely not. Kaufman was a common Amish name. Willa didn't want to believe that she had traveled all this way only to have her refuge crumble before she reached it.

John took the hamper from Willa's hands and stowed it under the back seat. "Nick Bradley got the call last night when he took me home after the safety meeting. He said his wife thought Ada was having another heart attack. He left my place to pick up Joshua and Mary and take them to the hospital."

"Miriam would want her daughter with her at such a time," Vera said.

Willa's hope that it wasn't her great-aunt faded. Ada had a daughter named Miriam and a son named Mark, but how was the sheriff involved with her family? Willa looked at John. "Is the sheriff related to them?"

"He is Miriam's husband. Mary is their adopted daughter," Isaac said.

"I don't understand." A chill settled in Willa's chest. How could her cousin Miriam be married to the English sheriff?

Isaac slipped his hands into the pockets of his coat. "It's an unusual story. Ada's daughter, Miriam, left the Amish and became a nurse after her brother died. The way I understand it, Ada and her husband were shunned by their church group because of Miriam's choice. They were members of an ultraconservative Swartzentruber church. I'm not sure where Ada came from originally. I think it was Millersburg, but Mary will know. Ada moved to Hope Springs and joined a more progressive Amish church so that she could see her daughter. When Ada's health began to fail, Miriam came home to take care of her. One night, someone left a baby on Ada's doorstep. Can you believe that?"

Willa pressed a hand to her throat. Had some other poor woman heard the voices that weren't real and done something she regretted? "Perhaps the babe's mother was ill and didn't know what she was doing."

Isaac shook his head. "She knew. Mary was a homeless and destitute child herself, barely sixteen years old. She thought she was doing what was best for her child by giving her away. Miriam and Sheriff Bradley tracked down Mary and reunited her with her baby. Not long afterward, Miriam married the sheriff and they adopted Mary. A few years later our son Joshua met and fell in love with both mother and daughter. That is how Mary and Hannah came to us, and we thank *Gott* daily for that blessing."

Willa struggled to keep her expression blank. Her great-aunt and her cousin Mark were both gone. Miriam was all the family Willa had left, and she was married to the sheriff. Willa didn't dare go to them.

Willa slowly backed against the buggy door as the conversation continued around her. What did she do now? There was no one left to help her.

She was truly alone.

Chapter Ten

Something was wrong.

John saw Willa shift to the back of the group as more people heard the news about Ada and gathered around Isaac for information. John worked his way to her side. Her starkly pale face frightened him. "Willa, are you all right?"

Her hand trembled as she grasped his arm. "Can we go?"

"What's wrong?"

"I have a headache."

It looked like more than a headache to him. Did this have something to do with the death of Ada Kaufman, or was it the baby? The wildness in her eyes worried him.

"I'm tired, that's all. I need to lie down," she said before he could voice his questions.

He grasped her elbow. "I will take you inside, and you can lie down there."

"I'd rather go home unless you wish to visit longer."

"*Nee*, I'm ready to leave." He opened the back door of the buggy and helped her inside.

He caught Samuel Bowman by the arm and spoke quietly into his ear. "Willa needs to return home. Can you help me hitch up?"

His eyes widened in alarm. "Of course. Should I send Rebecca to you?"

Samuel's wife, Rebecca, was widely known as a lay nurse. "*Nee*, Willa wants to go back to the house. She has been ill recently, and I think she is overtired."

"I'll go get your mare."

Vera seemed to notice what was going on and came to John. "Is Willa okay?"

"She says she has a headache and is tired. Will you fetch the girls?"

She nodded and made shooing motions to the people standing in front of the buggy talking to Isaac. They quickly made way and Samuel soon came trotting up with Clover. He and John made short work of hitching the mare. John climbed into the driver's seat as Vera reappeared with Megan and Lucy. He held his door open. "Sit up here with me, girls, and I'll let you drive after a while."

"Bless you," his mother said in relief.

She got in back and John slapped the reins against Clover's rump. The mare trotted quickly down the lane.

John glanced over his shoulder frequently as he drove home. Willa kept her face turned to the window. He couldn't be sure, but she looked on the verge of tears. He wanted to help, but he had no idea what to do. His mother patted Willa's hand and spoke softly to her. Willa answered but kept her face turned away. He couldn't hear what they were saying.

"Are you feeling better, Willa?" he asked after they had traveled a mile.

"I'm sorry to ruin everyone's day."

"You didn't ruin anything," his mother assured her.

Megan tugged on his sleeve. "I drive horsey?"

He had promised the child only to keep her and her sister quiet so they wouldn't bother Willa, but he didn't mind showing Megan what to do. Some of his earliest memories were of his father helping him to hold the reins on the way home from church.

"You will have to sit on my lap so that I can help you and you can see where you are going."

"Okay." He was surprised that she agreed. He lifted her up and settled her against his chest.

She eagerly reached for the reins and he showed her how to hold the lines properly. "You must keep the right amount of tension on them. Not too firm and not too slack."

Her hands weren't big enough to hold them correctly, but she concentrated on doing exactly as he instructed. When their first turn was coming up, he said, "Check your mirrors. Is there any traffic behind us?"

She stretched her neck to do so. *"Nee."*

He glanced back at Willa to see if she had heard her daughter use a *Deitsh* word. She didn't appear to be paying attention. That was unusual. She was always aware of what her children were doing and saying.

He helped Megan guide the mare around the corner. When they were straightened out again, Megan beamed a bright smile at him. "I did it, John. I drive *goot.* Clover *es goot gaul.* Right?"

It was the first time Megan had sought his attention or his approval. The tender emotions that flooded his chest pushed a lump into his throat. He swallowed hard before he could speak. *"Ja, liebchen,* you drive *goot."*

"I wanna do it," Lucy said, standing up to crawl into his lap with Megan.

"One at a time," he said. "Megan, can Lucy have a turn?"

For a second he thought she would argue, but she relinquished her place without a word. Lucy took the reins and jiggled them. "Giddy up, giddy up."

He stopped her from shaking them. "*Nee*, we are going fast enough. The horse has a long way to go. She will be tired if you make her run."

Lucy sat quietly for a while, but she soon lost interest in driving and wanted to sit with her mother. Willa leaned forward to lift her over the seatback. She held her hand out to Megan, but the child shook her head and remained beside John.

"I hold baby Henry," Megan said, looking up at him.

He would have liked to see that. "Did he cry?"

"*Nee*. Him *goot* baby. John like baby?"

"Sure, I like babies, when they aren't crying. Did you meet other new children today?"

Megan was soon telling him all about her friends and the games she had played. He was amazed at how talkative she had become all of a sudden. Was this the same distrustful child who'd called him "bad man" before today?

"Don't bother John, Megan," Willa said in a low, tired voice.

"She isn't bothering me," he assured her quickly.

Willa fell silent and continued to stare out the window as she held Lucy. When they arrived at the house, Vera took charge of the twins while Willa went inside. John put away the buggy and stabled the horse. When he entered the house a short time later, he found his mother in the kitchen alone.

"Can you open this for me?" She handed him a pint jar of canned chicken.

He twisted the lid enough to loosen it and handed it back. "Where are the girls?"

"I put them down for a nap. I'm making some chicken and noodle soup for supper. It will perk up Willa in no time." It was the meal she always fixed when someone in the family was under the weather.

"And where is Willa?" he asked.

"She went out the back door just a minute ago. Will you check on her?"

That was exactly what he needed to do. He opened the door at the rear of the kitchen and looked out. Willa, wrapped in a quilt, sat in the white wooden rocker at the far end of the porch with her head back and her eyes closed. She looked small, sad and vulnerable. A powerful urge to take her in his arms and kiss away her sadness made him realize how much this woman meant to him. He'd never expected to feel this way after losing Katie. He wasn't even sure his feelings were real. He wanted to believe it was just sympathy for the sad young mother, but he knew it was something more.

Willa rocked back and forth trying to calm her churning thoughts. Her headache had become a throbbing reality.

Dear God, what do I do? Help me, I beg You.

"Are you feeling better?" John's voice startled her.

She opened her eyes to see him sitting on the porch railing, watching her. The concern on his face tempted her to lie, but she couldn't. "Not really."

"Want to talk about what's wrong?"

Looking out over the snow-covered ground, she shook her head. "Not really."

He folded his arms across his chest. "Are you going to make me guess? Because if I had to guess, I'd say that Ada Kaufman was the great-aunt you were on your way to see."

Her gaze snapped to his. "How did you know?"

"You aren't very good at hiding your feelings."

That almost made her laugh. "I'm better than you think I am."

Otherwise he would see how much she had come to care for him.

"Why didn't you say something to Isaac about being related to Ada? I know Mary and Joshua. They would welcome a long-lost cousin with open arms."

"You are forgetting one thing. Mary's mother, my cousin Miriam, is the wife of the sheriff. I can't tell them who I am. He will enforce the *Englisch* law that says I'm an unfit mother and give my daughters to Glen's parents."

"You can't know that. Nick has great respect for our Amish ways."

"He isn't Amish, and neither is my cousin now. I can't trust that they will help me." Her voice caught in her throat.

"What will you do now? Will you go back to your grandfather?"

"I can't unless I know it is safe. The private detective employed by Glen's parents is an expert at tracking people down. According to what the sheriff told you, he has already discovered that I left the city by bus. He may have discovered where my grandfather lives and that I went to see him."

She had tried not to draw attention, but people noticed her daughters because they were twins. Their white-blond hair and vivid blue eyes made them memorable. She had tried keeping their heads covered with knit caps whenever they went out, but Megan was forever pulling hers off. The ticket agent at the bus station must have remembered them. The woman had commented that she had twin granddaughters about the same age.

Willa had seen the detective only once. Glen had spotted him loitering near their apartment building and pointed him out. She'd seen a small nondescript man with dark glasses, not the monster Glen told her was after them.

Glen had been furious because he had landed a good paying job at the local racetrack only two weeks before. They hadn't been able to return to the apartment until well after dark. They'd crept in, packed up their things and left that night. Glen died a month later. She had moved twice after his death, but it became much more difficult without him.

John scuffed one boot back and forth on the porch floor. "Nick told me that your trail disappeared where you got off the bus. I could ask him what more they know about you."

She shook her head. "It would only make him wonder why you're curious."

"I will finish the sleigh for Melvin Taylor before long. I could speak to your grandfather after I deliver it."

Willa sat up straight. "Would you? When will you go? It has to be soon. My baby will be here shortly after the New Year. I have to have a home for my children before then."

"I can have the sleigh finished in a little over a week. I will hire a truck to haul it next Wednesday and bring me back the same day."

She laced her fingers together. "John, that would be wonderful. I pray he has changed his mind and will shelter us."

"You must remain with us until I speak to your grandfather and return with his decision."

"It seems I have no choice. I'm sorry to impose on your kindness. I hope you know I'm grateful. Please let Grandfather know about Ada's death, too. They were estranged, but she was his sister."

John cleared his throat. "There is something else to consider."

"What's that?"

"You could stay in Bowmans Crossing permanently and make your home here. You already have friends in our community, for I consider myself your friend and so does my mother. God went to a lot of trouble to bring you to us. If your being here is His will, perhaps you should accept it."

John had no idea how tempting his suggestion was. To live in this community, among friendly and caring people, it was everything she had dreamed of finding for herself and her daughters.

She rubbed her hands up and down her arms. The one problem with the plan was that she had to confide in someone about her condition. As much as she wanted to tell John the whole truth, she couldn't bring herself to reveal what she had done in the past. She glanced at him. He wouldn't understand and she couldn't bear to see the revulsion on his dear face if he learned how she had tried to harm her babies.

"What do you think of that idea?" John asked.

She read the hope in his eyes and turned away. "It's a temping thought, but I want my children to be with family this first Christmas without Glen."

"Of course."

She heard the disappointment in his tone. It mirrored her regrets. If only there was a way for her to stay.

Maybe she didn't have to reveal those details. Maybe it would be enough to tell him she had been ill after the twins were born and that she could become ill again and might have to go away for a while. Would he accept that? She knew without a doubt that he and Vera would take care of the girls.

The midwife would have to know. Willa was prepared to share her history with a medical caregiver. The psychosis had come on with no warning last time. Someone needed to be ready to step in if it happened again. The midwife might even know of a place Willa could stay after the baby came if the worse happened.

Since the Amish didn't use insurance, Willa wouldn't have to provide proof of her identity if she had to be hospitalized again. The hospital would take the word of a midwife and treat the Amish woman Willa Lapp. The church would cover any medical bills she couldn't pay.

Then she remembered there would have to be a birth certificate filled out for her child. She would have to list the father's name or say he was unknown. To deny Glen was the father of her baby was unthinkable. How could she do that to his memory? How could she do that to her son or her daughter? Yet the detective might know about her pregnancy. Were birth records public records? Could he find the name she was using and the area she lived in by searching them? She wasn't sure. She wasn't even sure whom she could ask. Perhaps the midwife would know.

Willa rose to her feet and crossed the porch to lean on the railing beside John. Maybe he was right and this was God's will. Her detour to Bowmans Crossing may have been a blessing in disguise. She wasn't sure that the detective knew about her Amish upbringing, but in the event that he did track her as far as her grandfather's home, the trail would end there.

Her grandfather wouldn't offer information to an out-sider, but he wouldn't lie for her. The detective might learn from her grandfather that Willa Chase had gone to Hope Springs, but Willa Chase had never arrived at her great-aunt's home. Ada Kaufman was gone now. Only her daughter, Miriam, knew Willa. If questioned, Miriam would say she hadn't seen or heard from her cousin. The detective would believe her because it was the truth and because Miriam was married to the sheriff.

Willa was afraid to give voice to the hope that she might be free at last. "If my grandfather won't take us in, I'll consider staying."

John took her gently by the shoulders and turned her to face him. "As a friend I only want what is best for you and for your children."

"To have your friendship means a great deal to me, John. I cherish that gift, and I hope you know that you have my friendship, too." He was dearer to her than a friend, but she couldn't let it become anything more.

He smiled and gently covered her hand with his own. "Friendship is a gift meant to last a lifetime. For my lifetime, you shall have it."

He nodded toward the door. "Let's go tell my mother you are staying until I can return from delivering the sleigh. She's going to be thrilled. She might even tell me where she hid the carriage bolts."

Willa chuckled; thankful he could change the subject so easily. "I'm still not convinced she took them. I wouldn't know which ones to remove."

"She was married to a blacksmith for forty-seven years. She knows exactly which ones to take out and which ones to leave. She could probably make them for you."

"Now you are exaggerating."

"Actually, I'm not. She made all the cabinet pulls in the house because she didn't like the ones *Daed* made for her. Are you feeling better?"

"Much better, *danki*."

"Don't tell *Mamm* that until after you have had some of her special chicken and noodle soup. She thinks it can cure anything."

Willa smiled, but she knew chicken soup wasn't going to mend the ache in her heart. She cared deeply for John, but she could never allow herself to love him or any other man.

Chapter Eleven

Vera's eyes sparkled when she heard the news from Willa. "This is *wunderbar.* I have so much to do before Christmas and now I will have you to help me."

"Only for another week or so," Willa cautioned her.

"If that is *Gott*'s will. I must ready my Christmas cards to send and I need to get this house clean before my daughter and her family arrive. I'm not sure I have enough time even with your help, Willa."

John shook his head. "Christmas is a month away."

"You are right. I don't have a moment to waste. Where did I put the cards I got last year? I don't want to overlook anyone. My poor fingers ache at the thought of all those notes I must write."

Willa smiled indulgently at John's mother. "Perhaps I can assist you with that."

"You are a sweet child. I appreciate any help you can give this old woman. *Gott* will reward you for your kindness. I think I left the cards in a shoebox under my bed." She went off to search for them, leaving Willa and John alone in the kitchen.

"I knew she would be happy about it," he said.

"Her attitude makes me feel less like an intruder in the family."

"Never feel like that. There are many things you can do that will make her life easier. I have been thinking about hiring a girl to help her. Are you interested in the job?"

"Perhaps for my room and board, but not for a salary."

"I think a salary might be cheaper than feeding you. I've seen how much you can eat."

She was happy that he could tease her. She wanted to remain friends. "That reminds me, I'm hungry, John-john. Where is that ham you promised me?"

"I can see I'll have to slaughter another hog before the New Year."

"That would be wonderful, but what about right now?"

He tipped his head to the side. "Do you really want some ham? I can go down and bring it up."

She laughed. "No, I want pickles and peaches."

"Are you serious?"

"Very. Never make fun of a pregnant woman's cravings. I could want fresh bananas. How long would it take you to fetch some of those?"

"The local market isn't open on Sundays. You would be out of luck until tomorrow. That is if they had any fresh produce delivered in the snowstorm."

"Aren't you glad I only want canned peaches?"

"Good thing I brought up a half dozen jars of them yesterday. How many are left?"

"One."

His mouth dropped open. "You ate five quart jars of peaches?"

"Don't be silly. Your mother made two peach cobblers to take to church this morning. I've only had two jars."

"That's a relief. I was afraid I'd have to put a lock on the cellar door."

"You know we Amish believe in sharing everything."

Vera came back into the room with a shoebox in her hand. "That's the first time I've heard you refer to yourself as Amish. Are you ready to commit wholeheartedly to the faith?"

Was she? Could she take her vows with a pure and sincere heart?

"It can't be about hiding, Willa," John cautioned.

"Pray about it before you decide and let *Gott* guide you," Vera said, setting the box on the table.

"Either way, you will be welcome to remain with us," John said.

"I think I would like to speak to the bishop as soon as possible." Baptism was a serious undertaking, and she didn't want to enter into it lightly. From having listened to his sermon, Willa was hopeful that Bishop Beachy would prove to be a wise spiritual advisor.

"And the midwife," Vera said, taking a slip of paper from her pocket. "I took the liberty of obtaining her phone number for you. Our phone hut is a few hundred yards south of our lane. John can show you."

Willa inclined her head and took the paper. "I will visit the midwife here if I can't return to my grandfather's home, but I would rather wait until I know something for certain. I will write to Bishop Beachy tomorrow and ask him to see me. Will you be able to watch the girls for me if he can? I want my grandfather to know I'm seeking baptism."

"I would love to have them to myself," Vera said. "They can help me make Christmas cards."

Willa looked at John. "May I borrow your buggy?"

He leaned close to his mother. "She wouldn't have to use ours if her own could be fixed."

His mother lifted the lid off her shoebox. Four long metal grease-covered bolts lay on top of a sheet of newspaper. "Will you look at this? How do you suppose these got under my bed?"

Willa pressed a hand to her lips to hold back a laugh.

John plucked the bolts out of the box. "Someone who should confess her deception to the bishop put them there. You may take your own horse and buggy wherever and whenever you wish, Willa. I'll have it fixed first thing in the morning. I'll add a slow-moving-vehicle sign on the back as well as reflectors, turn signals and lights while I'm at it."

As he went out the door, Willa clasped her hands together and tried to look stern. "Vera, how could you do such a thing?"

The elderly woman gave her a smug smile. "It's quite easy if one has the right tools."

Over the next few days, Willa and the girls fell into an increasingly comfortable routine. They had breakfast with John and Vera. After John went out to work in the smithy, Willa and the girls helped Vera with the household chores. If the weather was nice, Willa let the twins play outside. Every hour that went by without the return of the sheriff allowed Willa to relax a little more. Often Vera would teach them new Amish words as they helped her with her cleaning or cooking. In the evenings after supper, John would read aloud from his Bible. The girls enjoyed climbing onto his lap and helping turn the pages. Willa caught him staring at her one evening and smiled at him. He looked away quickly as a dull blush crept up his neck. He was such a kind and gentle man. His easy way with her daughters endeared him to Willa as little else could do.

The following afternoon, the girls came running into the kitchen and grabbed Willa's hands. "Come play hide-and-seek, Mama," they said together.

It was their favorite game: a game with a purpose Willa hoped would someday be a part of the past. She was tired of running and hiding. "All right, we'll play."

"Can *Mammi* Miller play, too?" Lucy asked.

Willa looked at Vera. "What about it?"

"I thought you would never ask." She put her hands over her eyes and started counting.

John was in his smithy making a list of things he needed to finish Melvin's sleigh when the outside door opened. He looked up to see Willa come in. "What are you doing out here?"

She quickly closed the door behind her and grinned at him. "I'm hiding."

He chuckled. "Hiding from your girls?"

"From your mother."

"What is she up to now?"

"We're playing hide-and-seek with the girls. Your mother is very good. She has found me four times already."

"I didn't know she possessed such skill."

Willa crossed to the window to look out. "Neither did I or I wouldn't have invited her to join the game. Here she comes. Where can I hide?"

He moved his chair aside. "Quick, get under my desk if you can."

"I may be pregnant, but I'm still flexible." She dropped to her knees and crawled under it. He sat down and picked up his pen.

The outside door opened and his mother charged in. "Come out, come out, wherever you are."

He kept his head down, knowing he would burst out laughing if he looked his mother in the eyes. "Have you lost one of the twins?"

"I haven't lost anyone. I know Willa is in here." She moved around the room, looking into the corners and behind the forge. "Where is she?"

He turned in his chair to face her. "That's for me to know and you to find out."

His mother arched one eyebrow and leaned to the side to peek under his desk. "Like that, is it? Very well, she may win this round, but I'll win the game."

Chuckling, she left the smithy closing the door softly behind her. John held out his hand and helped Willa climb out from under the desk. Her face was flushed, and her eyes were sparkling as she stood. John didn't release her hand. Instead, he pulled her closer, driven by the need to kiss her. He stopped himself just in time. This wasn't the way a friend behaved.

Her smile vanished and her eyes widened as she gazed up at him. John stepped away from her quickly. "You can make it home safely now."

"*Danki.* You are always coming to my rescue." She sounded breathless.

"That's what friends are for."

"I'm grateful, my dear friend." She pulled her hand free, slipped around him and was out the door before he could think of anything else to say.

John kept busy over the next few days, working long hours on the sleigh for Melvin. Work in the smithy also kept him away from Willa except at mealtimes and in the evenings when the girls and his mother were present. Willa saw him as a friend, and he was determined to be that friend without asking for more. The problem was that he wasn't sure he wanted to settle for friendship. His feelings for Willa were growing stronger every day. It was foolish of him, knowing she could be gone in a few days.

He hammered home the brass tacks that lined the edge of the red velvet seat. It was the last thing he had to finish before he left in the morning.

For a long time he'd been unable to come to grips with losing Katie and their child. The arrival of Willa and her daughters had helped him do that. They had opened his heart to new relationships. If only a relationship other than friendship was possible with Willa. He wanted to ask her if there was a chance for something more, but in his heart he knew it was too soon.

The outside door opened and his mother came in. "I wanted to see this project before you hauled it away. It's beautiful. You have done a fine job on it."

"Danki." He looked over her shoulder. "Where is Willa?"

"I sent her to take a nap with the girls. She has been cooking and cleaning all morning. How are you getting along?"

He frowned. "What do you mean?"

"How are you and Willa getting along?"

He thought that was what she meant. "Fine."

"Fine as in you like her and she likes you, or fine as in it's none of my business?"

"You aren't very subtle."

She waved one hand. "I'm old. I don't have time to be subtle."

He sighed. She was like a dog with a bone. "Willa isn't a member of the Amish faith. I am. She still mourns her husband. Even if I were ready to consider remarrying, which I'm not, it wouldn't be possible."

"She is considering baptism. She wrote to the bishop and he has agreed to see her next week."

John put down his hammer. "She is not considering marriage."

"So she says. I wish she could see you for the *goot* man you are."

"She sees me as a friend."

"Many a marriage has started with friendship and grown into love."

"Don't hold your breath, Mother. You're old. You might not be able to hold it long enough."

"You make jokes, but I see your unhappiness."

He wished she wasn't so observant. "All things are as God wills. I leave it in His hands."

Willa watched John leave with the sleigh when it was finished with mixed emotions. She wasn't sure what news she wanted him to bring back. Was she to leave this place, or was she to stay? She kept busy during the day, but her eyes were frequently drawn to the window and the view of the lane. Near sundown she saw the truck turn in and went out to meet him. He waved to the truck driver as the man pulled away, and then he turned to her. A smile lit his tired face. Her heart grew light at the sight of it. How had she come to care so much for him in such a short time?

"Have you news for me?"

"I have plenty to share."

The front door of the house opened and his mother

stepped out. The twins came charging around her and attached themselves to his legs, forcing him to walk forward swinging each of them along as they giggled and shouted their welcome.

His mother wiped her hands on her apron. "You made good time. I have beef stew on the stove that is ready when you are."

"Sounds *wunderbar*. I will be in as soon as I have finished my chores."

She spoke to the children. "*Kinder*, leave the man alone and let him finish his work. Come inside and we will show him all the Christmas cards you have made after he has something to eat."

Willa stayed outside after the others went in. Her smile quickly turned to a worried frown. "Did you see my grandfather?"

"I did. Come into the barn while I finish my chores."

"Is my grandfather willing to take us in?" Willa asked.

"He has not changed his mind." John looked down. "To my way of thinking, it is for the best. I can't see the twins growing up in Ezekiel Lapp's dour household."

Willa sighed and followed him to the barn. "I thought he might change his mind after he learned that his sister is gone. Has anyone been there to ask about me?"

John stopped inside the door to face her. "Melvin said an *Englisch* fellow visited all of the farms in the neighborhood. Melvin knew I gave you a lift to your grandfather's place."

Her eyes widened with fear. "Then he will come here looking for you."

"He won't. Melvin didn't care for the man's attitude and decided not to tell him anything. He said the man was pushy and rude to Mrs. Taylor. Melvin was happy to hear you are safe with my family."

"I remember Melvin as a kind man."

"Is Chase your real name?"

"It was my married name. I went back to using Lapp after Glen died. Maybe that wasn't very smart, but it's a common enough name among the non-Amish, too. Did the *Englisch* man speak to my grandfather?"

"He tried, but your grandfather wouldn't talk to him. According to Melvin, that was the reception the man got at most of the Amish farms he visited."

"What did my grandfather say when you told him about Ada?"

"Sheriff Bradley and his wife had already been there to inform your grandfather of his sister's death. Your grandfather did ask Miriam about you. When she said she had not seen or heard from you, he assumed you had gone back to your *Englisch* life. He didn't tell her that he had sent you to Ada."

"When you told him I hadn't returned to my old life, was he happy about that? Did you tell him that I'm considering baptism?"

"I did. He said he no longer has a granddaughter, and he asked me to leave."

She turned and leaned against Clover's stall. So that way was closed to her forever.

John moved to stand behind her. "You know what this means?"

"It means I have no family."

He laid his hands on her shoulders. "It means you may stay among us without fear of discovery. No one knows you are here."

She turned around and wiped the tears from her

cheeks with both hands. "I will always fear discovery. Glen's parents won't stop looking. The sheriff is a friend of yours. We will run into him somewhere someday. He'll overhear the girls talking and realize they aren't Amish children. It's a short leap from that to wondering if I'm the missing woman with twins that he's been looking for."

"Have faith, Willa. God is with you and your children. He led you here for a reason."

Willa wanted to believe John. She wanted to believe God brought her to these people to find sanctuary among them, but she couldn't let go of her fears.

Her baby would be born in a few weeks. She had nowhere else to go. She needed somewhere to live and someone to protect her children. "Is the invitation to stay with you and your mother still open?"

"You know it is. You have a home with us for as long as you want it."

"I don't have a choice. I'm sorry."

"My mother will be over the moon."

"And you?"

He placed one finger under her chin and raised her face to look at him. His lopsided grin tugged at her heartstrings. "I'm getting used to having you and the children underfoot."

She looked away from the affection shining in his eyes. "I need to make an appointment with the local midwife, and I need to find a job."

She would need money if she had to run again, but she had no idea where she would go.

If the midwife couldn't shelter her, then John and Vera would have to know her secret. She prayed that would never happen.

* * *

Vera was delighted with the news. The following morning found her busy taking inventory of her baking supplies for the upcoming cookie exchange. "I must make plans for Christmas. It will be *wunderbar* to have *kinder* in the house on Christmas morning. There is so much to do. I'm sorry your grandfather has rejected you, Willa. I may write him a letter and tell him what I think of his coldheartedness, but I will wait until after Christmas to do so."

"I have forgiven him. He has suffered much in his life, and it has made him bitter."

"You put me to shame for my un-Christian thoughts of the man, but I may write anyway. Would you mind cleaning my good dishes in the hutch?"

Willa hid a smile. "Not at all."

Megan tugged on Willa's dress. "*Mamm*, can we play outside?"

"*Ja*, but stay on the porch."

Willa finished wiping off the good dishes displayed in Vera's hutch and paused to listen. The girls had been playing outside on the porch after their nap, but the sounds of laughter and chatter had stopped. She glanced out the window. They were nowhere in sight, the pail and spoons she had given them to play with lay on the steps. Pulling a black shawl from a peg by the door, she wrapped it around her shoulders and stepped outside. She couldn't see them.

"Megan, Lucy, where are you?" They didn't answer.

She walked around the side of the building to check the garden. They weren't there, either. A seed of worry sprouted in her chest. Where were they? She scanned the snowy landscape. All she saw was a yellow barn cat hunting along the garden fence.

She called again. The cat stopped and glanced her way before leaping over the fence and running off. Willa started to turn back to the house but noticed two sets of twin-size footprints in the undisturbed snow beside the fence. They led through a side gate in the garden.

Perhaps they had gone down to John's workshop. She hoped that they weren't annoying him. He had been surprisingly patient with their questions and pestering.

The snow between the house and the barn had been churned by numerous horses and boots during the past two days. Willa couldn't distinguish the children's footprints, but she suspected they were heading to the barn to look for the kittens. They liked to feed them milk when John did his chores. Gray clouds drifted across the face of the sun, blocking much of the warmth. She pulled her shawl tighter around her, wishing she had chosen her heavy coat instead.

John's workshop was empty; however, the glow of coals in the forge proved he had been working there recently. Both buggy horses were still in their stalls, so he had to be nearby. She started to call out to him but paused when she caught the distant sound of childish laughter.

She moved through the dark barn toward the far door. It was open and she stepped through. The sun came out from behind the clouds. The dazzling brightness momentarily blinded her. She cupped a hand across her brows to block some of the light.

Her girls were both with John. He didn't look annoyed in the least. He stood with her daughters on top of a low earthen dam at the head of a small pond in his pasture. Each of her daughters was seated in a shiny aluminum grain shovel. They squealed with delight as John pushed first one and then the other down the snow-packed incline and out onto the ice, where they whirled around a time or two before falling over.

"Again," Megan shouted as she jumped to her feet.

Lucy tried to stand but slipped and sat abruptly, giggling all the while.

Laughing, John walked out onto the ice to set Lucy upright and onto her shovel. Then he pulled both girls back up to the top of the dam.

Willa leaned her shoulder against the doorjamb to watch them. The shovels were the same kind of makeshift sled her father had used when she was small. Spinning across the ice in one was among her fondest winter memories. When she was older, her father had given her a real sled. It might have gone farther and faster, but it never twirled her around until she was too dizzy to stay upright the way her father had done.

"There you are. You'll catch your death out here in nothing but a shawl." Vera draped a coat across Willa's shoulders.

Willa snuggled into the warmth. "I just stepped out to check on the girls. I didn't intend to be out here long."

"Did you find them?"

"They are with John. They seem to be having a very good time." She nodded toward the pond.

Vera stepped to the barn door and stood beside Willa. "*Gott* be praised. I was beginning to think I would never see that again."

"A child on a scoop shovel?" Willa grinned as John folded his large bulk onto one shovel and let Megan and

Lucy try to pull him across the ice. They didn't make any progress until he helped by pushing with one hand.

"Nee."

Willa heard the catch in Vera's voice and glanced at her. "Then what?"

"My son happy and laughing the way he was before Katie died." Vera pressed a hand to her trembling lips as tears glinted in her eyes. "I'm so glad you and your *kinder* came to us."

Not knowing what to say, Willa slipped her arm around Vera's shoulders and hugged her close. The two women stood watching the merrymakers for another few minutes, then Vera pulled away. "You should get back to the house before you freeze."

"I will in a minute." Willa didn't want to go in. She wanted to watch her little girls being carefree and happy. They were probably too young to remember this day when they were her age, but maybe God would allow this happiness to stay with them and outweigh the sadness they had known.

Vera leveled a stern look at Willa. "If you aren't back in the house in ten minutes, I'll send you to bed without your supper."

"I'll come in, I promise."

"See that you do." Vera's expression grew serious. "Don't hurt my son. He's grown fond of you and your girls."

Willa looked at her in surprise. "Vera, I would never knowingly hurt either of you."

"I reckon it's the unknowing hurt that I'm most worried about."

She walked away, leaving Willa to stare after her wondering what she had meant by her cryptic remark.

Chapter Twelve

It snowed heavily during the night, and the following morning arrived overcast and cold. Willa knew she had put off calling the midwife long enough. After breakfast she bundled up the twins and trudged with John to the end of the lane and down the highway to where a small red building sat back from the road in front of a stand of cedar trees. A solar panel extended out from the south side of the roof. Through the window in the side of the building she could see it was unoccupied. She opened the door and stepped inside.

The shack held a phone, a small stool and a ledge for writing materials along with an answering machine blinking with one message. She looked at John. "Shall I listen to it?"

"Sure. I use it for my business, as do my neighbors. Just don't erase it if it isn't for me."

It was for him. Melvin Taylor had referred a man to John for an estimate on restoring a wooden bobsled. John wrote down the man's number. "I'll call him when you're done."

A local phone directory hung from a small chain at

the side of the ledge, but Willa didn't use it. She had the number for the midwife on the piece of paper Vera had given her. The woman answered on the second ring. Willa answered a few questions, made an appointment and hung up. Afterward, she and the girls threw snowballs at the cedar trees while John conducted his business. When he came out, they all started home together.

The girls ran ahead of them, stopping occasionally to throw a snowball at unsuspecting objects. Lucy threw one and a rabbit darted out from beneath a clump of grass at the base of the fence post. She squealed in delight. "Mama, see bunny run? Johnjohn, what's bunny called?"

"The bunny *es der haas*."

"I see *der haas*," Megan said, looking to him for confirmation.

He took his hat off and plopped it on her head. *"Ja, der schnickelfritz saw der haas."*

Willa laughed. "*Schnickelfritz* is the perfect description. A mischievous child is exactly what she is. They're both mischievous children."

His smile was warm as he looked down at her. "I think they must take after their mother in that way."

"Perhaps a little," she said as Megan ran down the road with his large hat wobbling on her head.

"Perhaps a lot. When do you see the midwife?"

"She can see me Saturday at noon."

"I can drive you if you'd like."

"That won't be necessary," she said quickly.

"I don't mind. You shouldn't go alone."

She hated to point out the obvious problem with his offer. "I appreciate that, but it wouldn't be wise. I don't want to start any talk about us."

He looked taken aback, then blushed a deep shade of red. "I see your point. My mother will drive you."

"I will drive myself. End of discussion."

The girls came running back to them as Lucy tried to snatch John's hat from Megan. "Help me, John," Megan shouted.

"I want hat, Johnjohn." Lucy pouted when she couldn't catch her sister.

John stood up straight and raised his hands like claws. "The big bad *beah* wants his *hut*. Grrr." He charged toward them, sending them shrieking as they dodged away from his swinging arms. Finally, the make-believe bear snatched them both up, whirled around once and toppled backward into a snowbank.

Willa chuckled as she picked up his hat from the roadway where Megan had dropped it. John had an amazing way of lifting her spirits and making her want to laugh aloud. He could make her grin without even trying. What was it about this man? She tried to put her finger on it, but she couldn't. Happiness had been such a foreign emotion since Glen's death that she almost didn't recognize it.

Looking away from his infectious grin, her gaze traveled to Megan and Lucy. Not only could John make her smile, but her daughters appeared to be falling in love with him.

Willa bowed as she handed his hat to him. "Your *hut*, sir *beah*. Please don't eat my *schnickelfritz*."

"Oh, that sounds delicious. I will have *schnickelfritz* for lunch." He snapped his teeth at first one twin and then the other.

The girls scrambled out of reach and ran toward the house, calling for Vera to save them. Willa extended her hand to help John to his feet. He got up without assistance and began to brush the snow from his clothes.

Willa folded her arms and watched him. "I want to thank you, John."

"For what?"

"For befriending my daughters. They miss their dad. You are making it easier for them." She reached up to brush a lingering patch of snow from his shoulder.

"I'm glad I can help. Have I made it easier for you?" His voice held a low breathy quality that made her look at him sharply.

"I can't think about me. I have to think about them and what they need." She started to turn away, but he caught her by the arm.

"You will have to think of Willa Lapp sooner or later."

"Perhaps, but not now." She gently pulled away from him and followed her girls into the house.

A little after eleven o'clock on Saturday morning, Willa hitched up her horse and drove over to her appointment with the midwife. The midwife's home was a modest old farmhouse painted white just off the highway four miles from the Miller farm. If not for the power lines running to the house, it could have been the home of an Amish family.

Willa liked Nurse Willard as soon as she met her. A tall, big-boned woman with short gray hair, Janice, as she insisted on being called, was a no-nonsense woman who valued plain speaking. She wasn't happy with Willa for waiting so long to consult her and for failing to bring her medical records.

After Willa's exam, Janice wrote in a manila folder

while Willa got dressed. "If your prepregnancy weight is accurate, you could stand to gain a few more pounds."

"John says I eat all the time."

"Ignore him. Is that your husband?"

"I'm a widow. My husband passed away last May. I'm staying with John and Vera Miller."

Janice folded her hands. "I'm sorry for your loss."

"Thank you."

She went back to writing. "Your official due date is January 11, is that right?"

"Yes."

"That makes you thirty-four weeks and a few days. Are you sure about your dates?"

"Pretty sure."

"Don't be surprised if you don't go to forty weeks. You mentioned you have twins. Were they delivered by C-section?"

"I delivered them naturally."

"You were a fortunate woman. Twins can be tricky to deliver, especially for a first-time mother. Any complications during your pregnancy?"

"None."

"What about afterward?" Janice asked without looking up.

"Is this conversation confidential?"

That caused the midwife to put her pen aside and face Willa. "It is. So are your medical records and personal information. I'm a nurse-midwife, and I'm bound by the laws of this state to keep what you tell me in strictest confidence. I can't share any of your information without your written consent."

Willa couldn't look the woman in the face. She stared

down at her clenched hands. "I had an episode of post-partum psychosis after the twins were born."

"I see. You must have been terribly frightened by that."

"I didn't know what was happening. I don't remember much, only what I was told."

"Did you receive psychiatric care?"

Willa nodded, unable to speak.

"Were you hospitalized? What treatments did you receive, what drugs?"

"I don't have any of those records."

"If you tell me where you were hospitalized, I can get them."

"I'd rather not say."

"Mrs. Lapp, you have had a serious complication that could reoccur. I am not an expert on this illness. I have to know how to help you. I understand you are staying with Vera and John Miller. Are they aware of your condition?"

Willa looked up. "I don't want them to know. They won't understand."

"You aren't giving them enough credit. The Amish in this area are progressive. Bishop Beachy has openly urged his congregation to seek help for mental health issues, both from within the church and from outsiders if need be."

"The stigma is still real no matter what they claim. I've seen it. My parents were driven out of their church because of my mother's depression."

"I'm sorry that has been your experience. Willa, what were your symptoms? How did your psychosis present?"

"I would rather not say."

"Okay, but you are going to have to work with me. When did they start?"

"When the twins were two weeks old."

Janice sat back in her chair. "A home delivery is not out of the question, but you will need close monitoring for several months. Have you thought about how you will explain that to the family you are staying with? This is a small community. Word gets around."

"I was hoping to deliver here and stay here. If the Millers or the community have to be told anything, I will tell them I became sick after the twins were born and I might become sick again and have to be hospitalized."

"I do have a delivery suite and a recovery room where mothers and fathers can stay overnight, but I'm not equipped to have a long-term patient here. You would need around-the-clock observation."

"I have to stay somewhere. I can't burden Vera Miller with my care."

"She can arrange for mother's helpers to stay with you. You won't burden Vera."

"And then everyone in the community will know I'm being watched in case I turn crazy." Willa couldn't keep the bitterness from her voice. How many whispers had she heard about her mother? How many pitying looks had she endured even after they left the Amish? The English world had been no better in spite of her father's hopes. She didn't want to put her girls through that. She didn't want to put John through the same confusion and pain Glen had endured as he tried to cope with her insanity.

Janice crossed her arms and leaned back in her chair. "I'd like your permission to speak to several of my colleagues about your case. One is the doctor I practice under, Dr. Marksman. He will have to be informed. The other is also an RN, so your privacy will be protected. Her name is Debra Merrick. She is the public health nurse in our district. I'm going to ask her to line up professional mental health help for you in the event it is needed. We will find a place for you to stay. Although you aren't an abused spouse, we do have a home for women in need that's run by a Christian women's charity. I'll speak with them. We'll work something out."

"Thank you." Willa forced herself to relax.

"Try not to worry. I'll have Dr. Marksman and Debra here to meet you at your next appointment, which will be the twenty-first of this month. That will put you at thirty-six weeks. I see all my mothers weekly for the last month, so plan on coming in weekly until you deliver. We will figure out the best thing to do for you and your baby."

Janice walked Willa to the door. Before she opened it, the nurse-midwife turned to Willa. "I strongly advise you to confide in someone. You can't do this alone. Your condition is not your fault. You shouldn't be ashamed. You would not be ashamed if you broke your arm after falling on the ice or suffered an attack of appendicitis."

How could it not be her fault? There was some flaw in her that she should have been able to control. "My mind is made up. I don't want anyone outside of the doctor and the other nurse to know."

"Then that is what we will do."

Willa walked outside and climbed into her buggy. If she managed to get past this delivery without people learning about her condition, she would be safe from then on out. There would not be another pregnancy because she would never remarry. At least not until she was past her childbearing years. Then and only then would she be able to think about her own desires. About her feelings for John.

He was attracted to her. She would have to be blind not to see it. Would he be willing to wait for her? It would mean he'd never have children of his own. No, she couldn't do that to him.

John was waiting just inside the barn for Willa when she drove up. He came out to take her horse, impatient to know that she and her baby were okay. "How did your visit with the midwife go?"

"The baby and I are both well, but she said I need to gain more weight before I see her again."

"That must have made you happy. I'm going to get a lock for the refrigerator."

Willa smiled, but it didn't reach her eyes.

"What else did she say?"

Willa got out of the buggy. "Not a lot. I have to see a doctor next time."

"A doctor? Why?" He stared at her over the back of her horse.

"When the twins were born, I became very sick and had to be hospitalized. There is chance that could happen again. The midwife wants to take some precautions."

"What kind of precautions?" How serious was it?

"I may have to stay near a hospital for a few weeks after the baby is born."

"A few weeks?" He'd never heard of a new mother needing to stay away from home for so long.

"Just to be on the safe side."

It was odd that she didn't look at him. Was she embarrassed to speak of such things? "I'm sure she knows best. Have you spoken to my mother about this? *Mamm* may know of some remedy for this ailment."

"I haven't. As I said, it's a precaution and my worry may be for nothing. You know how I like to worry. You have told me to have faith. I want you to know I'm trying. I'm going to go see the bishop tomorrow evening to talk about getting baptized. I'd rather not go alone. Would you come with me? I would ask your mother, but I'm hoping she will watch the girls for me."

He was pleased that she wanted him beside her. If she chose to join the faith, there wouldn't be anything keeping them apart. He would be free to tell her how much he had grown to care for her. "I'd be happy to drive you."

Willa had a hard time concentrating on the preaching during the church service on Sunday morning. Was she making the right decision? She prayed that she was. Happily her girls were well behaved, and she had to take them out only once. At the meal, she barely picked at her food, sparking a frown from Vera. The long morning was finally over, but Willa's soul searching continued.

She hid her nervousness as she rode beside John in the buggy on Sunday evening. She wanted to make the right decision, but she wasn't sure what that would be.

If she chose to join this church, she would be bound by their rules for a lifetime. Living without electricity wasn't the most difficult part of being Amish, although she did still reach for the nonexistent light switch when she entered a dark room. Living without the convenience of a phone, traveling by horse and buggy, and wearing plain clothing didn't trouble her. Opening her home to any Amish person who needed assistance would be a chance to repay the kindness she had received. What did trouble her was the knowledge that she might be making her decision based not on her love of God but on her fear of discovery.

The true meaning of becoming Amish wasn't in the outward signs of the faith. It was about committing her life to God as a member of a pious community. It was about giving her life over to His will.

The sheriff hadn't returned. That gave her hope that she had been accepted at face value and he wouldn't come looking for her again. The midwife had a plan to make sure Willa and her new baby would be safe if the need arose. If bringing Willa to Bowmans Crossing was God's plan for her sanctuary, then she had to let go of her lingering fears. If only it wasn't so hard.

The bishop's wife showed them both into her husband's study and returned a short time later with refreshments. Willa had her choice of coffee or spiced apple cider and a number of delicious-looking cookies and cakes. She chose the spiced cider and a pumpkin roll.

The bishop came in a few moments later. "I see my wife, Ellie, is already plying you with food and drink. Welcome, Willa Lapp. I see by the note you sent that you are interested in joining the faith. Can you tell me why?"

Willa drew a deep breath and started her story. "My *Englisch* husband passed away, and I am alone in the world except for a grandfather who will not accept me and my children into his home because my parents were shunned. I thought I had other relatives in Hope Springs, but I have recently learned that they have passed on or have left the church."

"I'm sorry to hear this. We welcome you to get to know our community. I'm sure you have learned a great deal about us from John and Vera."

She smiled at John. "I have. Their kindness to me and my children is a big part of my decision to remain in Bowmans Crossing. Everyone I have met only reinforces those feelings."

"I'm pleased to hear that. Tell me about your Amish childhood."

"I was raised in a Swartzentruber Amish community. I had completed my baptism classes but had not yet been baptized when my parents left the community. I was only fifteen and my mother was ill. I thought we might come back, but my parents wouldn't allow me to return. My parents died within a year of each other. Mother died first. I still thought we would go back to our community then, but my dad wouldn't consider it. He became ill a short time later. I stayed to take care of him. When he died, I wrote to my grandfather, but he never replied. I was alone."

The bishop listened to her, nodding occasionally.

"I soon met and fell in love with a good man and we married. We had twin daughters the following year. Then my husband was killed in a hit-and-run car accident."

Ellie reached over to cover Willa's hand with her own. "God has given you many trials."

"Your path back to us was not an easy one," John said quietly.

It hadn't been easy, but he was right. Every turn in Willa's life had brought her closer to this place and these people. And to God. If she believed that, she had to believe that this was where she belonged. This was God's plan for her. This was where she was meant to serve Him. A deep calm spread across her mind as she opened her heart to His will.

The bishop took a sip of his coffee before speaking. "We normally hold baptism classes twice a year. In the fall and in the spring."

"I am aware of those practices," Willa said.

"Candidates attend nine meetings with our church leadership over a two-and-a-half-month period leading up to the baptismal ceremony."

"Since I have already completed the baptism classes, would it be possible for me to take my vows without repeating my instructions? I would be happy to allow the church leadership to test my knowledge and my conviction." She laid a hand on her belly. "This child is due in January, and I wish to be baptized before he or she is born."

Shaking his head, the bishop held up a hand to caution her. "This is not a decision to be rushed."

"I am not rushing into it. I made my choice many years ago. The right to take my vows was denied me. I lost my way because of that. I ask only for the chance to make my vows before God and the church so that I may bear my child with a cleansed soul and a joyful heart."

The bishop looked from Willa to John and then to his wife. He folded his hands together and considered her request. Finally, he nodded once. "This is a very unusual request, but I see no reason why I can't discuss this with our church elders. Your desire to serve God is heartfelt. I see that in your eyes. The ministers and I are meeting tomorrow evening to discuss another issue. I will give you our decision the following day if we arrive at one."

Willa didn't realize she had been holding her breath until she had to speak. "*Danki*, Bishop Beachy."

"Are you planning to attend our cookie exchange?" Ellie asked.

"I am. May I have another piece of your delicious pumpkin roll? I do need the recipe."

Mrs. Beachy smiled brightly. "I'll write it out for you right now."

When Willa left with John a half hour later, snow had begun to fall. Willa's breath rose into the air in a frosty cloud. She couldn't remember the last time she had felt so lighthearted and free. She held her arms wide and opened her mouth to catch snowflakes.

"Was it the right decision?" John asked.

She clasped her arms around herself to hold on to her joy. "Oh, John, it was. I've never been so sure of anything in my life. Even if I can't be baptized before my baby arrives, I will be baptized with the next class in the spring."

"I'm happy you can consider staying until spring."

Willa drew another deep breath. "I wish I could say I'm not worried about being discovered. I am. But each day brings me more peace of mind. Can you feel Christmas in the air?"

"What?"

"Christmas is coming. The night our Savior took the form of a tiny baby to bring Salvation to us all. Isn't it glorious?"

"You are making me wonder what Ellie Beachy puts in her pumpkin roll."

Willa chuckled. "Offhand, I would say she adds a generous dose of Christmas spirit. Let's get home. I want to make some tonight."

He opened the buggy door for her to climb in. "As long as you promise not to eat them all yourself."

"John Miller, you begrudge me every bite I take."

"I don't, but Clover may. She's the one that has to pull you around." When he climbed in, the buggy sagged in his direction. He outweighed her by over a hundred pounds.

Willa folded her arms. "No pumpkin roll for you."

On Friday afternoon, a buggy carrying four members of the church leadership arrived at the Miller home. Willa waited patiently in the background as Vera made them welcome and settled them in the living room. When he was ready, the bishop beckoned Willa to take a seat on a chair facing the men.

One by one, they took turns asking her questions about the faith and about her understanding of the eighteen articles of the Dordrecht Confession and if she had read them. She had when she took her baptismal classes, but the German words had carried little meaning for her at fifteen. She had read them again from the prayer book Vera loaned her with an English translation. It left her with a better understanding and respect for the traditions of the Amish church and an abiding belief in the articles of faith.

They then asked her if she understood what was expected of her according to the church's *Ordnung*. Vera and John had spent many hours detailing the church rules for her. She didn't remember them all. She stumbled when she listed them and thought her hopes of being baptized were lost, but Bishop Beachy simple smiled. "Some members are better than others at knowing the rules and following them. The congregation is reminded of the *Ordnung* twice a year."

"Can you live by these rules?" one of the ministers asked.

"I have lived with them and I have lived without them. I freely choose to live by them for the rest of my life."

When asked if she could shun a wayward member by the deacon, Willa hesitated.

"I understand the need to shun a person who willfully disobeys the church laws. It is done out of love, to make them see they have sinned and to bring about a change of heart. I would have to be sure they had been given every chance to repent and return before I voted to place them under the *Meidung*. Having seen how deeply it can divide a family, I would, but I would never be eager to do so."

After two hours, the men retired to John's bedroom for a discussion. Willa's hands were shaking when she went to the kitchen sink for a drink of water.

"How is it going?" John asked from the back door. Willa read the encouragement in his eyes. He had the girls with him. They looked tired.

"I have no way of knowing. Are you girls ready for a nap?"

Megan nodded. Lucy shook her head but rubbed her eyes with both hands.

John leaned against the doorjamb. "They may not be tired, but I am. I can't swing a shovel around one more time without my arms falling off."

"You are good to keep them occupied."

"You must know I will do whatever I can to aid you."

The tenderness in his voice brought tears to her eyes. "You are the best friend I've ever had."

"The look in your eyes says you see more than a friend just now. Why can't you admit it, Willa?"

"I have to put the girls down for a nap." Willa headed them toward their bedroom, determined not to look at John again. She did see more than a friend. She saw in him the man she was growing to love. As hard as she had guarded her heart against him, he had found a way in. As she opened the door to the girls' bedroom, the door to John's room opened, too, and the men came out.

Bishop Beachy leaned down to speak to the girls. "Who have we here?"

"I'm Lucy. Megan's my *shveshtah*." Lucy rubbed her eyes again.

"I see you have learned one *Deitsh* word since you have been with us."

Megan gave him a sour look. "*Der katz, a milchkuh* and her *kalbs* stay in barn. What's bunny called?"

Bishop Beachy laughed heartily. "The bunny *es der haas*."

Megan smiled at him. "*Ja ver goot.*"

He chuckled as he looked at Willa. "It seems that I have been tested and have passed, as have you. Because of your heartfelt desire, you will be baptized on Sunday the nineteenth before the service."

When the men left, Vera wrapped Willa in a big hug. "I'm so happy for you."

"I can't believe it."

Vera stepped back and rubbed her hands together. "We have very little time. We must take you around and introduce you to as many families as we can before Sunday so everyone feels comfortable with you joining us. Those who meet you will love you as much as John and I do. Isn't that right, John?"

"It is hard not to love her." He opened the back door and went out.

Chapter Thirteen

"**I**'m going to need a job." Willa kneaded the bread dough while Vera looked on with a cup of coffee in her hand. Willa found the rhythmic movements were soothing. Over the past two days, she and Vera had been in and out of the buggy too many times for Willa to recall. She had met over two dozen of the local families. Once they finished the bread, they would be on their way to Isaac Bowman's home for a meeting with his family, as they were hosting the service where Willa would be baptized.

"You have a job. You take care of me, your *kinder* and John."

"I don't take care of you or John. You can both take care of yourselves. Besides, I need a paying job. I will need to get a place of my own someday. Any suggestions?"

"Add a little more flour to the dough if it feels sticky."

Willa sprinkled a handful on the table. "I don't mean the dough, I mean about finding work."

"I think the bread dough has been kneaded enough. Go ahead and divide it into the pans."

"I'm serious about finding work, Vera." She would need money if she had to get away quickly. For now, she had to pray God would be merciful and keep her hidden, but she wanted to be prepared if someday she had to leave.

"You know you are welcome to stay with us. You can't leave until after the babe is born."

"I know." She didn't want to leave. Every day she discovered some new thing about John that made her care for him more. Harder still was knowing he cared for her, but she didn't dare return his affections. Perhaps living apart would lessen her affection for him.

"If John is the reason you don't want to stay, you can tell me now."

Willa shrugged. "Maybe he is part of it."

"He's a stubborn man. Sometimes he can't see what is right under his nose, but he will make a good husband. If you gave him a little more encouragement, it might make a difference."

Willa shaped the dough in the pans and turned to face Vera as she wiped her hands on her apron. "You mistake my meaning. I'm fond of John the same way I'm fond of you, but I don't want to encourage him. I'm not looking for another husband."

"You should be. You're young. You have children to care for. You don't have to remain alone. Would your husband want that for you? I think not."

Glen would have wanted her to be happy, but that was beside the point. She wasn't able to be a wife. "I'm content to raise my children and live a good life. I don't need a husband for that."

"Harrumph," Vera said in disgust as she pulled open

the oven door so Willa could slide the bread pans in. "John isn't the only stubborn one in this house."

"Who says I'm stubborn?" he asked from the doorway. Neither of the women had heard him come in.

"I do," his mother said, shooting a sharp glance at Willa. "And so is this one."

"I thought that the first time I met her. I'd like to show you something, Willa. Can you come out to the workshop?"

She couldn't think of a good excuse not to go with him. "Sure."

He looked over his shoulder. "Where are the girls?"

"Playing with their dolls in their room. Shall I get them?" Willa was already moving in that direction. With the twins around, she could avoid the pitfalls of being alone with John.

"*Nee.* I don't want them following us. I need your opinion on something."

Willa had no idea what he was talking about, but she put on her coat and followed him out to the smithy. He checked behind them, then he picked up a bundled object from the corner and carried it to the forge. He pulled off the burlap wrapping. "What do you think?"

It was a toddler sled. Only, this one was big enough for two. The curved rails around the back that kept a small child from rolling off backward were metal and painted bright red.

"John, it's lovely. Did you make this?"

"The base is pine. It should hold up through a few years of use. They will outgrow it quick enough, but your next child can use it, too."

"The girls will love it."

"Do you think it's too fancy for a Christmas present?"

"With the red paint? A little, but they are so young they won't know any different. You are always doing something kind for them."

He stepped close. "It's because I like their mother. I'm trying to win her affection by currying favor with her children."

She looked away. "I wish you would stop. It won't do you any good."

"I was afraid you would say that. Perhaps this will change your mind." He placed a hand beneath her chin and lifted her face to his. Slowly, he bent low and kissed her.

Willa had time to move away, but her feet wouldn't listen to her brain. The tenderness of his lips against hers made her respond in kind. Her mind stopped shouting that it was a mistake and her heart took over. She cupped his face with her hands and lost herself in the sensations his touch brought to life. It was a wonderful, tender kiss unlike any she had known before.

He groaned and pulled her close. It wasn't until her belly bumped against him that her foggy mind started working again. She pushed against his shoulders and turned her face away. "You must not do this."

"Not do what? Not show you that I'm falling in love with you? I've been trying to hide how I feel, but it's a losing battle."

"I have to go in."

He gripped her arms. "Why must you run away? I know you mourn your husband, but I am the man you were kissing seconds ago. You can't tell me otherwise."

"Please, John. I can't do this. Do I care for you? Yes, I do, but there can never be anything between us."

"Why? What is holding us apart? Your children? The

babe you carry? Is that what worries you? Willa, I can love them because I love you."

She shook her head and gazed into his eyes. "I don't need to explain myself to you. I'm sorry to hurt you. I never intended to do that, but you have to forget this happened."

He dropped his hands to his sides, freeing her. She stumbled toward the door, brushing away the tears that sprang to her eyes. Behind her he said, "I'll forget this kiss the day after you do, Willa Lapp."

Willa went in the house and straight to her room. She didn't want Vera's eagle eyes to see the traces of tears on her face. When she had washed her face and regained her composure, Willa came out of her room and saw Vera taking the last loaf out of the oven. Lucy and Megan sat at the table enjoying warm slices of bread with butter and sugar sprinkled on it.

Vera glanced at Willa. "Oh, *goot*, you are ready. John is bringing round the buggy."

Willa's heart sank. "John's not coming with us, is he?"

Vera's eyes narrowed. "He is. Does it matter?"

"Not at all," she said with a forced smile.

When the girls were finished with their snacks, Willa helped them into their coats and sent them out to sit up front with John. She took her spot in the back seat and avoided looking at him for the short drive to the Bowmans' home. She pressed a hand to her mouth as she remembered the feel of his lips against hers. Why had he kissed her? Why had she kissed him back? It had been foolish.

The Bowman house was set back near the river. A small shop boasting Amish gifts and crafts above the door was located just off the highway. Past the gift shop, a large metal building contained the woodworking and furniture-making business the Bowmans were renowned for.

Of the Bowman family, Mary and Joshua were still gone, but Isaac and Anna welcomed Willa, as did the rest of their sons and their wives.

Isaac slipped his thumbs through his suspenders. "So you have decided to stay in our district. What made you change your mind? I thought you were on your way to Hope Springs."

Willa looked down. "I learned my family no longer lived in the area. It had been many years since I was in touch with them. Since I was really looking for somewhere to settle with my daughters, I felt Bowmans Crossing was as good as any and better than most."

"It is indeed." Isaac turned to John, who was standing by the buggy. "I have some work for you if you are interested. Can you look at the shaft on my lathe and tell me what it will take to fix it? It's out of balance."

Anna and Vera went inside. Rebecca gave Willa a hug. "Have you met our nurse-midwife yet?"

"I did. I see her again next week."

"Isn't she a fun lady?"

"We haven't gotten to know each other well enough for me to say. She was nice and seems to know her job." Willa was still hopeful that Janice would be able to secure a place for Willa to stay after the baby was born. Knowing she might have to stay with Vera and John weighed heavily on Willa's mind, but at least she knew Lucy and Megan would be well cared for.

"I forget you haven't known Janice as long as I have. If you haven't already arranged for a mother's helper, I can give you the names of a couple of local girls. They were both wonderful during the month after Henry was born. I didn't have to lift a finger if I didn't want to."

Willa followed Rebecca inside the house. "More than a mother's helper, I need a job."

"Are you serious? Isn't your baby due in a few weeks?"

"Yes, but I can work until then, take some time off and return after the baby arrives. I have no money of my own, and I have lived off the charity of the Millers far too long already."

"I might be able to help."

"Really?"

"We are short-handed at my mother-in-law's gift shop. The holidays are our busiest time of the year, and with Mary still in Hope Springs, we have been struggling to cover for her."

"I've worked in retail before."

"Can you run a computer?"

"Until I'm baptized. Was the computer question a test?"

"Not at all. We have permission from the bishop to use computers for our businesses only. They are powered by our generator and use Wi-Fi to connect to the internet by satellite. It sounds like I know what I'm talking about, but I can't even turn the thing on, let alone fill orders. Isaac has an *Englisch* teenager that handles most of it, and she's barely seventeen. Are they born knowing this stuff now?"

"Do you honestly think I could get a job here?"

"I'm almost sure of it. Let's go see what Anna has to say. I think she'll jump at the chance to hire you."

Rebecca led the way to the kitchen, where Vera and Anna were chatting with several other women.

Willa stopped Rebecca before she went in. "Will I be able to bring my daughters to work with me? They are only three years old, but they are well behaved." She didn't feel safe leaving them alone all day. It would take time to adjust to having them out of her sight.

"I take Benjamin and Henry with me and they are not well behaved. Your children will be welcome."

As Rebecca predicted, Anna was thrilled to have an experienced worker offering to hire on for Christmas and even afterward. She went out to get Isaac to decide on a salary. His offer was generous by Willa's previous work standards, but Rebecca assured her that all of them earned the same amount. Willa had a job starting tomorrow. Everyone congratulated her.

Anna clapped her hands together. "Enough chitchat. We have work to do."

"What work?" Willa asked, looking at the smiling women around her.

"We are going to make your baptismal dress and there is no time to waste."

Together, the women measured, cut and stitched together a new black dress, a black organdy *kapp*, a lovely new white cape and a long white organdy apron for the occasion. Willa was overwhelmed and grateful for their generosity.

She waited for John's comment about her job as Vera told him on their way home later that afternoon. He looked at her for a long moment. "If this is what you wish, I'm happy for you."

He didn't sound happy. She avoided facing him across the supper table during what would surely be an awkward meal by pleading a headache and staying in her room. The next morning, he was gone by the time she got up. She dressed and fed the girls. Vera made them a lunch to take and handed the brown paper bag to Willa. "Don't spend the whole day on your feet. Put them up when you can and drink plenty of water."

"I will. Don't worry about me."

"You girls mind your *mamm*," Vera told them. "I don't want to hear bad reports about you. Are you sure you don't want to leave them with me?"

"They have never been away from me for so long. I want them to feel comfortable and see what I'm doing before I leave them with you for the day."

"They would be fine, but you are their *mudder*. Get a move on, girls."

"Okeydokey," Megan said.

Lucy whirled on her. "I say okeydokey. Not you."

Megan pouted but didn't talk back. Vera shook her finger at them. "This is not the way to start your mother's first day on the job."

Willa wondered at the tension between the girls but didn't have time to deal with it. She left Vera to get them into their coats and went out to hitch up her horse.

John had her mare hitched and waiting when Willa stepped outside. He tipped his hat to her and went inside the smithy without a word.

She had allowed her weak will to destroy their friendship. She should have found a way to avoid his kiss without hurting his feelings.

The store was busy, but Willa had no trouble keeping up with the flow of customers. Many of the Amish ones just wanted to visit with each other. Many of the *Englisch* ones bought items, but most wanted to snap pictures of the twins in their *kapps*, which Willa discouraged. All day long as she worked, Willa wondered what the coming evening was going to be like when she returned home. She couldn't very well plead another headache and continue to hide in her room. Vera would march her off to the doctor if she did. Would John remain aloof? Would he avoid spending time with the girls?

When she reached home an hour before suppertime, the girls charged through the door ahead of her. John was waiting in the living room with his paper open. He quickly folded it shut and held his arms wide. "My *schnickelfritz* are home. *Kumma*, tell me about your day."

They crawled into his lap and began chattering about the store and how baby Henry threw up on his *mamm*'s shoe. Willa was so grateful for his continued friendship with the girls that she couldn't speak until she swallowed the lump in her throat. "You have a *goot* friend in John, girls."

"I know." Lucy nodded vigorously, kissed his cheek and snuggled against his chest. Willa turned away and went down the hall because that was exactly what she wanted to do, too.

"Have you forgotten our moment together? I have not," John called after her.

She paused with her hand on the doorknob of her room and sighed. "Try harder."

Chapter Fourteen

John had no idea how to break through the wall of Willa's reserve except to pound away at it as he did with the hardest steel in his shop. Brute force wasn't the answer. Metal had to be tempered, heated to the melting point and worked before it grew too weak or too hard again. He already knew he had to melt Willa's resistance, and her daughters were the fire he would use.

"Can the girls stay home with me today?" he asked at breakfast two days later. Willa had those dark circles under her eyes again. She wasn't sleeping well. Part of him was glad and part of him hated to be the cause of her discomfort.

"That will be fine. I think they are getting bored with playing behind the counter. Even baby Henry is losing his luster."

"Where women are concerned, it happens to all men," he said sadly. "Some of us sooner than others."

He was rewarded with a hint of a smile. "Some men never had much luster to begin with."

"True. When do you have an appointment with the midwife?"

"Next Tuesday."

"Will you have trouble getting off work to go?"

"*Nee*, for Rebecca has said she will cover for me."

"Have you gained enough weight to make the midwife happy, or should I put a brick in your pocket?"

That brought out a real smile. "One brick or two? I have the feeling she will scold me if I gain too much."

"One brick, then, or another jar of peaches?"

She met his gaze for the first time in days. "I do have a craving for peaches."

"I'm glad to hear that. I'll loan you the money to buy some at the gift shop. I don't want the midwife to think I'm starving you."

He heard her laughter behind him as he walked out the door to hitch up her horse, feeling exceedingly pleased with himself. They might not be back to where they were before the kiss, but this was a start.

When the second hymn finally came to an end on Sunday, Willa entered the house of Isaac and Anna Bowman and took the seat reserved for her near the minister's bench. She sat with her head bowed on this most solemn occasion. She was vowing to reject the world, accept Jesus as her Lord and live a humble life in a community governed by God's word.

The ministers and the bishop entered the room from behind her. For the next several hours Willa listened to the sermons delivered first by the ministers and then by the bishop. She tried to absorb the meaning into herself. She closed her eyes and breathed deeply. This day she felt the warmth of God's presence. She gave thanks for the goodness He had bestowed upon her and begged His forgiveness for all her doubts.

The bishop finally ended his sermon and turned to Willa. "The solemn vow you make today is not made to me. It is not made to any of the congregation here with us today, for we are only witnesses."

He raised his hand and pointed to the ceiling. "This vow you make unto God Himself. Let there be no misunderstanding. Let no doubt remain in your heart."

The deacon came forward with a pail of water and a cup. The bishop looked at Willa. "Is it your desire to become a member of the body of Christ?"

"It is my heart's desire," she answered firmly.

The bishop's wife came forward and untied the ribbons of her *kapp*. The bishop then laid his hand on Willa's head. "Upon your faith, which you have confessed before God and these witnesses, you are baptized in the name of the Father and the Son and the Holy Spirit. Amen."

The bishop cupped his hands over Willa's head. The deacon then poured the water into the bishop's hands. It trickled through his fingers and over Willa's hair and face.

The bishop then extended his hand to her. "In the name of the Lord and the Church, I extend to you the hand of fellowship. Rise up and be ye a faithful member of our church."

Willa stood. The bishop gave her hand to his wife, who greeted her with a Holy Kiss upon her cheek.

Facing the congregation, Bishop Beachy said, "It is the duty of everyone present to aid this new member as we would each other. We must be ever watchful that none of us strays from the path God has set before us.

All must conform to the *Ordnung* of this church without question. Though these rules are sometimes difficult, they are made for the good of the many and not of the one. Obey them and never depart from them."

Willa glanced at John and saw tears upon his face as he smiled with joy for her.

On their way home late that afternoon, Willa heard Vera speak softly to John. "She is baptized. I've held my breath long enough. I'm not getting any younger."

The following afternoon, John came in from finishing his chores to find his mother spooning cookie dough onto a baking sheet and singing a Christmas carol. Slightly off-key but with enthusiasm. The twins sat on the kitchen floor banging on pans with wooden spoons and occasionally joining in with a word or two. Loudly and very off-key.

"O Holy Night" had never sounded quite so bad. John stood in the doorway to the kitchen and stared at his mother in amazement. He couldn't remember the last time he had heard her voice raised in song outside of church services or the last time she had looked so happy.

She caught sight of him and fell silent. Her smile faded. When she stopped singing, the girls stopped banging. She pushed the last spoonful of dough onto the sheet. "I thought you were out in your workshop."

"I just came in to see if there was any coffee left from supper."

"Johnjohn, we go carol."

"That's right. We are going caroling tonight."

The cellar door opened, and Willa came up with several quart jars of fruit in her hands. "Are these the ones you wanted?"

His mother took the jars from her. "They are. There isn't any *kaffi* left, but I'm sure Willa can fix some. I wouldn't mind having a cup myself."

"I would be happy to make some," Willa said quietly, keeping her eyes averted.

"Don't go to any trouble on my account." He wished she would look at him more often.

"Sing more, *Mammi* Miller," Lucy said, banging her pot.

"That's all the singing for now. Put your pots away," his mother said.

Megan frowned. "Aw, do we have to?"

"Yes, you have to." Willa held out her hand for the spoon.

He had certainly put a damper on their impromptu concert. His first thought was to leave and let them resume their fun, but something held him in place. He leaned his shoulder against the doorjamb. "I would like to hear more singing, *Mammi* Miller."

His mother folded her arms over her chest, leaving smears of flour on her sleeves. "You may choose the next song as long as you join in."

If she expected him to back out, he decided to disappoint her. She knew he didn't like to sing. "I will if Willa will. How's that for a tongue twister?"

He caught a hint of a smile before Willa subdued it. "Willa will if John joins in willingly. Say that three times fast."

"I think I'll just sing." He drew a deep breath and began, "Joy to the world, the Lord is come." His voice was often compared to a bullfrog, but he was going caroling tonight no matter what.

He motioned to Willa and his mother, and they

joined in. The twins started banging, and by the second verse they were adding a stream of *joys* to the lyrics. He glanced at Willa and found she was smiling at him. Today it reached all the way to her eyes. They sparkled with amusement, and it made him feel that he was making headway. Painfully slow headway, but they were moving in the right direction. Toward each other.

Two hours later, John waited beside Samuel's sleigh and tried unsuccessfully to curb his excitement. He was almost as giddy as Megan and Lucy. A sleigh ride with Willa at his side was his idea of the perfect winter evening, especially since he didn't have to drive. Lucy was the first one out of the house. She quickly claimed her spot in the front seat beside Samuel. Megan came out next and scrambled up beside her sister. He'd never seen them so delighted.

"Are you sure you don't want to sit in back with your mother?" John asked, praying they would say no.

Samuel winked at John as he covered the pair with one of the lap robes he held. "They will have a better view up here, and it won't be so crowded in the back seat. I remember what it was like to go caroling before I became an old married fellow."

John was thankful the darkness hid the blush he knew was staining his cheeks red as he climbed in the back seat. He would owe Samuel a favor for arranging this. *"Danki."*

"Don't mention it."

Rebecca came out followed by John's mother and Willa. Rebecca settled on the front seat with the twins between her and her husband. Willa stepped aside to let Vera get in beside John.

"I'm afraid I can't tolerate sitting in the middle,"

his mother said without a hint of shame. "I hope you don't mind."

"*Nee*, of course not." Willa took John's hand as he helped her in. He gave her gloved fingers a quick squeeze and saw her smile before she looked down.

Samuel handed several quilts to John. His mother got in but shifted uncomfortably. "Can you scoot over a little more, Willa? I'm practically hanging out the side."

John wanted to kiss his mother's cheek. He heard Samuel's laugh quickly change into a cough. John lifted his arm and placed it over Willa's shoulders as she moved closer. "Don't worry. I will keep you warm," he said in a low voice as he spread the robe over her.

Willa remained stiff as a metal rod beside him. As much as he wanted to pull her closer, he knew it would only make her more uncomfortable. It took time for heat to bend steel, and he was becoming a patient man.

"Is everyone ready?" Samuel asked. Five confirmations rang out. Samuel slapped the lines and the big horse took off down the snow-covered lane. Sleigh bells jingled merrily in time with the horse's footfalls. The sleigh runners hissed along over the snow as big flakes continued to float down. They stuck to the hats of the men, turning their brims white before long. Megan and Lucy tried to catch snowflakes on their tongues between giggles.

John leaned down to see Willa's face. "Are you warm enough?" She nodded, but her cheeks looked rosy and cold. John took off his woolen scarf and wrapped it around her head to cover her mouth and nose.

"*Danki*," she murmured.

"Don't mention it. In spite of the cold, it's a lovely evening to go caroling, isn't it?" The thick snow obscured the horizon and made it feel as if they were riding inside a glass snow globe. The fields lay hidden under a thick blanket of white. Pine and cedar tree branches drooped beneath their load of the white stuff. A hushed stillness filled the air, broken only by the jingle of the harness bells and the muffled thudding of the horse's feet.

Their first destination was only a mile from John's house. They reached it all too soon. As they drew close, he saw several sleighs parked in front of the home already. The other members of the Bowman family were waiting for them. They all got out and walked toward the house. The porch light was on. The front door opened to reveal his neighbors Connie Stroud and her daughter Zoe waiting for them. As Lucy and Megan scrambled down from the sleigh, John offered Willa his hand to help her out. When she took it, he gave her an affectionate squeeze. She graced him with a shy smile in return.

"Was this what you imagined Christmas would be like when you decided to return to your Amish family?"

She shook her head. "I never imagined anything like this. Do you do it every year?"

"We do."

"You aren't going to actually sing, are you, John?"

He threw back his head and laughed. "*Nee*, but I will hum along."

"Softly, dear, softly," she suggested.

He wondered if she realized that she had called him *dear*. It was turning out to be an even more wonderful night than he had hoped for. He squeezed her hand as the song began and softly hummed close to her ear.

They made stops at various English and Amish homes as the group made a circuit around the farms in the area. Wherever they stopped, they were greeted by cheerful people with hot drinks and mounds of cookies. Samuel called out the song titles and began each one as the group followed his lead. They sang five songs at each home before bundling into the sleighs again. Calls of Merry Christmas and *Frehlicher Grischtdaag* followed them when they left. Lucy and Megan were worn-out before the sixth house. John and Willa remained in the sleigh with the girls bundled under the quilts while the others sang.

He looked over at Willa. "I hope you don't mind missing out on the cookies."

"I don't when I have something so sweet in my arms." She adjusted Lucy's hat to cover her ears.

"I feel the same way." He hefted Megan to a more comfortable hold. "What will we do when we have three? We don't have enough arms between us."

"You should have children of your own, John," she said, looking away.

"I like yours. I can't wait to meet the next one. Are you hoping for a boy or a girl?"

"I would like a boy."

He pulled the quilt up higher around Megan and knew it was now or never. He had to share his heart, or he would burst. "I've become mighty fond of little girls and of one grown woman who happens to be their mother."

"I know the girls are fond of you, too."

"And their mother? How does she feel?"

"She likes you."

"There's a problem, then."

She glanced his way. "What problem?"

"I more than like you, Willa Lapp. In fact, I'm in love with you. What are we going to do about it?"

I'm in love with you. What are we going to do about it?
The question echoed through Willa's mind as she stared at the hope in his eyes. What could they do about their growing feelings for one another? She was in love with John. He loved her. She didn't doubt him, but what future was there for them? How could she make him see how hopeless it was unless she told him the truth? The whole terrible truth. She had tried to kill the little girls he loved.

She could do the same to another child. To the child she carried.

Show me the path I need to take, Lord.

John waited patiently for her answer.

She looked away. "I can't change how you feel, but I can't give you the love you seek."

Megan raised her head. "Can we go home now?"

"We'll go home soon," Willa assured her.

"Willa, talk to me," John said. "I know you care about me."

"Not here. Not in front of the girls."

"Then tomorrow. We need to talk without interruptions."

"I have to work until noon, then I see the midwife."

The carolers came back to the sleighs. Vera settled herself in the back seat and glanced at the girls. "These two won't be up in time to go to work with you, Willa. They can stay home with me. Anna has invited some of the schoolchildren and their families over tomorrow for treats. I'll bring the girls in to meet the children at noon and they can stay and play with the others."

"I'll bring them," John said. "That way you can get your grocery shopping done, and I can drive Willa to her midwife appointment."

"Wunderbar," Vera said, patting Willa's hand.

Willa forced a smile. She had until tomorrow to think of a way to let John down without breaking his heart. And hers.

Willa sighed as she dusted the jars of jam on the gift shop shelves. A sleepless night had provided only one answer. She had to tell John about her condition. Perhaps with the support of the midwife, Willa could make him see that loving her was pointless.

The bell over the front door jingled. "I'll only be a minute, Nick. I just want to grab some hard candy for Hannah."

Willa turned around, happy for the distraction. An English woman with dark auburn hair and bright green eyes walked across the floor toward her. She wore jeans and an emerald green parka that brought out the color of her eyes. There was something familiar about her.

"Do you have root beer candy? The kind that looks like little barrels?"

Her voice gave her away. Willa stared, unable to believe her eyes as her cousin Miriam Kaufman stood smiling in front of her. She was Miriam Bradley now. The sheriff's wife. Miriam hadn't changed much in ten years.

"We are out of root beer candy." She wanted to shout at her to go away.

The woman pointed to the display case. "No, you aren't. I see a bag right here." She tipped her head to the side. "Don't I know you?"

"I'm new here." Willa looked away, resisting the urge to run.

"Willa? It is you. Willa Lapp. Little cousin Willa. You are the spitting image of your mother. How long has it been?"

"Ten years, I think. How are you, Miriam?" Willa saw the sheriff step out of his vehicle as a tour bus pulled up beside him. He waited as a dozen tourists got off.

Dear God, please don't let him take my babies.

"It's been a hard month so far. My mother passed on a few weeks ago. Did you know that?" Miriam asked.

"I heard. I'm sorry." *Please go away. Stop talking to me.*

From the corner of her eye, Willa saw John pull up in his wagon. *No, no, no. Take the girls home, John.*

Willa wasn't sure she wasn't screaming the words aloud. Miriam turned and pointed out the door. "That's my husband. He's the sheriff. I never joined the Amish, but I guess you can see that for yourself."

The back door opened and Rebecca came in. "I see John is here. I'll take over for you, Willa."

"Danki." How could this be happening? John lifted Megan out of the back of the wagon. He hadn't seen the sheriff. Willa stripped off her apron and grabbed her coat from behind the counter. She couldn't meet her cousin's eyes. "Good to see you, Miriam. I have to go."

"We'll see each other again. My daughter lives here."

Willa wanted to run to the wagon, but she forced herself to walk. She passed the sheriff on his way into the building. He stepped aside and tipped his hat. "Good day, *Frau* Lapp. Nice to see you again." After what seemed like an eternity, she reached John's side. "I have to take the girls with me. Lucy, Megan, get in the buggy."

"I thought I was taking you to the midwife."

"My plans have changed. I have to go home." She untied the horse from the railing at the side of the building.

"Willa, what's wrong?"

"I can't talk." She got in her buggy, and as soon as she was out of sight of the gift shop, she whipped the horse into a run.

John got home as fast as he could. Willa's sweaty horse stood in front of the house. He had no idea what was wrong. He moved through the house calling her name. She didn't answer. He stopped at her bedroom door and saw her bundling clothes together.

"Willa, what are you doing?" John stared at the purple backpack on her bed.

She emptied the pegs on the wall and the drawers of her bureau and stuffed everything into her bag. "I have to go. They are going to find out where I am if they don't know already. I have to protect the girls."

"Who do you have to protect them from?"

"From Glen's parents. They will know where I am soon if they don't already."

"What are you talking about?"

She closed the bag and faced him. "My cousin Miriam came into the gift shop. She recognized me. She will tell the sheriff and he'll come for me and take the girls away."

"You aren't a bad mother. We will show Nick the truth."

She turned her back to him. "You don't understand. I once did something very wrong."

He stepped close behind her and laid his hands on her shoulders. "What are you saying?"

She leaned back into his arms for a brief instant. Then she straightened. "I have to go."

He turned her around. "Go where?"

Cupping his face in her hands, she shook her head sadly. "You can't help me. I can't tell you where I'm going. They will come here looking for me, and I don't want you to have to lie for me. But I want you to know that I do love you, John. Please forgive me. If you love me, you won't try to stop me."

"That's not fair."

"I do love you. Never doubt that. No matter what you hear about me, know that I love you with all my heart."

"You're coming back, aren't you? When these people find you aren't here, they will go away."

"I wish it were that simple. They won't stop looking for us."

"What about Megan and Lucy? How will you explain this to them? They have grown to love me as I love them. They have grown to love my mother. She adores them. Taking them away will break her heart."

"Please, John, this isn't easy for me. Don't make it any harder."

He caught her hand. "I don't want it to be easy for you. I want it to be impossible for you to walk away from me."

Willa's heart ached for the pain she was causing him. "If only you knew how close to impossible it is. I'm sorry." She barely choked out the words.

Picking up her suitcase, she pressed past him and into the hall. Her daughters were playing with their dolls on the living room floor. "Get into the buggy, girls."

A sharp pain cut across her abdomen. Willa gave a muffled moan and leaned against the chair back. "Not now."

"Where we going?" Lucy asked.

"We have to take a little trip." When the contraction let up, she knelt and helped Lucy button her coat.

Megan touched her cheek. "Mama is sad."

Willa sniffled once and wiped away the tears that slipped down her face. "I'm not sad. I was just out in the cold too long."

Megan looked over her shoulder. "John sad. Need hug, John?"

"Yeah, I need a hug." He dropped to one knee and drew both girls to him.

"You're squishing me." Megan pulled back in protest.

Lucy wrapped her arms around his neck. "Love you, Johnjohn."

"I love you, too." His voice trembled. He kissed the top of her head and then kissed Megan. "*Gott* be with you."

Willa pressed her hand to her mouth to keep from sobbing. Why had God brought her to this wonderful man only to tear her away from him? It was so unfair.

"Let's go, girls." She struggled to her feet and swung her backpack over one shoulder. If she waited another minute, she wouldn't have the strength to walk away from him.

She opened the door but didn't look back. "Tell your mother goodbye for me."

He didn't say anything. She stepped out and closed the door behind her.

Chapter Fifteen

John wanted to smash his fist into the door. How could she do this? How could she turn her back on what they had? On her vows to the church? What had she done that was so terrible?

He sank to the floor as tears rolled down his face. Why did she make him love her and then leave?

He couldn't imagine life without her or her wonderful children. He was starting to think of her baby as his own child. In his mind they were his family. It had been a foolish daydream and nothing more.

He was sitting alone at the kitchen table when his mother came in half an hour later. She pulled off her coat and bonnet and hung them up. "I'm sorry I'm so late. I was talking with Belinda at the store and the time just slipped away. Where is Willa?"

"She has gone." Saying the words aloud made them even more painful.

"Gone where?"

He looked up and met his mother's puzzled gaze. "She wouldn't tell me."

"John, what are you saying?"

He drew a deep breath and sat up straight. "Willa has taken the children and has left us. She won't be coming back."

"*Nee*, that can't be."

"I wish with all my heart that it wasn't true, but it is."

"Why?"

"Miriam Bradley recognized her. Willa fears Nick will take the girls away."

"And you let her go?"

He stared at the floor. "What could I do?"

"Anything but sit alone in an empty house."

He rose slowly to his feet. "You're right. I will be out in the smithy."

His mother took hold of his suspenders with both hands. "*Nee*, you won't!"

"*Mamm*, stop it." He tried to free her grip, but she held on.

"I won't stop until you hear me. You locked yourself in your smoldering world of grief and hammered away until you had a shield of iron around your heart—until Willa and her children broke through it. Your great regret was letting Katie drive away that day after your argument without trying to stop her."

"It's not the same."

"You're right. It's not. You can't change the past, but you can find Willa and the children before she disappears with them forever."

"How am I going to find her? She wouldn't tell me where she was going?"

"Use your brain. She will need a car to get far away quickly. Who would drive her? She has no money."

His mother might actually be right. "The public health nurse and the midwife both have cars. They might help her."

"Debra Merrick doesn't have a well-baby clinic today. She won't be at the school."

"Willa had an appointment with the midwife this afternoon."

"Go there. If you fail to find her, at least you will know you tried."

He bent and kissed his mother's cheek. "I'll find her and I'll bring her home."

John didn't bother with a buggy. He bridled Clover and swung up bareback. The shortest distance to the midwife's was through the woods by the river. He nudged the mare to a gallop and prayed his mother's guess was right.

Twenty minutes later, he saw two cars in the driveway along with Willa's buggy.

Please, God, let her be here.

He jumped off his horse, charged through the front door and skidded to a halt in the midwife's living room. Willa sat weeping on the sofa with Debra Merrick holding her hand.

Debra smiled at him. "Willa, I think you know this man. Lucy has mentioned you a lot, Johnjohn."

His racing heart slowed as he gazed at Willa's puffy eyes and tear-streaked face. He took off his hat, dropped to one knee in front of her and took her other hand. "No more running away, no more secrets. I'm here. I'm going to stay no matter what you tell me because I love you and I don't want to live without you."

Willa swallowed hard as she stared at his beloved face. "You won't feel that way when I tell you everything."

Janice came in from the other room. "The children are watching TV. You must be John Miller. Thank you for coming. Willa needs all the support she can get. Unfortunately, Dr. Marksman had an emergency."

John squeezed Willa's hand. "I'm listening."

She looked into his eyes, knowing the love she saw there would soon die, but he deserved to know the truth. "Two weeks after the twins were born, I developed what the doctors call postpartum psychosis. I started hearing voices. They weren't real. I know that now, but they were as clear to me then as your voice is today."

He raised one eyebrow. *"Narrish?"*

"I was crazy, yes."

"We don't use that word," Debra said. "You had a psychiatric illness."

Willa didn't take her eyes off John. "It's rare, but this illness happens only to new mothers. I never knew such a thing was possible. I was tired and depressed. The girls were fussy all the time. I felt like a failure as a mother. Glen said it was just the baby blues, but it turned into something much worse."

"Go on," John urged gently.

Willa drew comfort from his acceptance so far. "The voices told me to take my infants to the river and hide them in reed baskets so Glen couldn't hurt them. That shouldn't have made sense. He would never have hurt them, but I believed the voices. I don't remember what happened after I reached the riverbank. I was told I waded into the water with the babies strapped in their car seats, not in reed baskets. If I had let go of them, they would both have drowned. Do you understand? They would have died if a stranger hadn't stopped me from dropping them into the water. I was going to kill them, and I didn't even know it." She buried her face in her hands and started sobbing. Every day she gave thanks for the woman who had saved the lives of her daughters.

Debra spoke again. "Postpartum psychosis is caused by hormonal changes in a woman's body after she gives birth. It affects about one out of a thousand women. Sadly, we know little about how the brain is affected. We do know that approximately half of women who have had one episode will have another episode with their next pregnancy."

"But half of them will not be crazy again," John said.

"As I said, *crazy* isn't a word we use, but that's correct. The good news is that this condition can be treated. As I have been telling Willa, now that you and she are aware of the possibility of a reoccurrence, you can take steps to minimize the risks."

"What kind of steps do we take?" he asked.

Willa's gaze snapped to his. "We?"

His troubled expression faded. "You are not alone. You do not have to face this without help."

"You heard what I said. What I did."

"I heard you, and I have heard these women. The burden God has given you to bear is beyond my understanding, but not beyond my love."

Janice laid her hand on Willa's shoulder. "John is right. You aren't alone. That is the beauty of belonging to an Amish community. The incidence of postpartum depression is lower among Amish women. Studies suggest the reason is because Amish women have so much help after a new baby is born. Family members and mother's helpers arrive to take over the new mother's chores and leave her free to rest and focus on her baby. Getting adequate rest is one way to decrease the risk of a psychotic episode occurring. Another way is the use of antidepressant medication. The third step is to decrease your stress. Part of that means accepting help. This isn't something you have to hide. We will all help you."

Willa wiped her cheeks with both hands. "I can't stay. My husband's parents are trying to take my children away from me. They claim I am an unfit mother. They may know where I am by now. I have to get away."

Janice pulled up a chair and sat beside Willa. "You are not an unfit mother. I had no idea you were dealing with such an emotional issue. You must be terrified. Have you spoken to an attorney?"

Willa shook her head. "My husband didn't trust them. He said we had to keep moving so that his parents couldn't find us."

Debra patted Willa's hand. "I'm not one to speak ill of the dead, but he was wrong about that. It is difficult for grandparents to gain custody of their grandchildren in this state. Our courts are very reluctant to remove children from their biological parents. It is unlikely that your in-laws have been granted custody without an investigation and documentation of abuse or neglect."

The first bit of hope sprang to life in Willa's heart. "Are you sure? Glen said they have the money and influence to take the children from us."

Debra sat back. "I can't be positive, but I am certain of one thing. You are not an unfit mother and you should welcome the chance to prove it. I know several child welfare workers in this county. They can assess the children's home situation and prepare a report for your attorney. You do need a lawyer, and I can recommend a fine one. She's a friend of mine. With your permission, I will speak to her about your case. I'm sure she will help."

Willa looked to John. "Is that acceptable?"

He nodded. "It is to me."

Debra and Janice exchanged pointed looks. Janice said, "There is a way to make certain they can't remove the new baby after he or she is born."

"How?" John asked quickly.

Janice glanced from Willa to John. "In Ohio, when a woman marries, her husband is recognized as the legal father of her unborn child even if he is not the biological father. Your in-laws would not have a claim on the baby when he or she is born. Adoption is the only way you can gain legal rights for the twins."

John rose to his feet and paced across the floor as he considered Janice's words. If he proposed to Willa now, would he be placing undue pressure on her to wed him? He wanted her to marry him because she loved him, not because it would put her baby beyond the reach of her in-laws. He turned to gaze at her. God willing, they would have many years to sort out their feelings on the subject. "Willa Lapp, will you marry me?"

John didn't wait for her answer. He closed the distance between them and took her hands in his. "Let me do this."

She pressed a hand to her forehead. "I don't know what to say. I need to think."

"*Nee*, don't think." He wrapped his arms around her and gently kissed her, savoring the feel of her in his embrace. A rush of love for her pushed away his doubts and left him overwhelmed with tenderness for the courageous woman he held.

She pulled away. "I love you, John, but I can't let you do this."

"I love Lucy and Megan. You know that. I couldn't love them more if they were my own. Your babe is already the child of my heart. Why not let me give him or her my name?"

"I don't want you to marry me in haste and regret your decision for years."

"I won't regret it."

"What if I become ill again? What if I say terrible things and do terrible things each time I have a baby? You would soon learn to hate me."

"Never." He gripped her hand. "Marriage is for better or for worse, in sickness and in health. We don't know what God has planned for us, but I want a future with you if He allows it. A future we'll face together. I can speak to the bishop right away. We have both been married before, so we may wed at any time. This must be your decision, Willa. Place your trust in God and in me, and do not allow fear to rule your heart."

He watched the struggle going on behind her eyes. She closed them and bowed her head for so long he began to lose heart.

Chapter Sixteen

"I don't deserve your love, John." Willa looked up and smiled at him. "But I have never been more grateful for anything in my life."

"Will you marry me?"

"I can't believe you still want that."

He gathered her in his arms. "I will never stop wanting you, Willa darling. Give me the right to keep you by my side for as long as God wills. Give your children the right to call me their father."

"What if we lose them?"

He kissed her cheek. "We won't. I have faith in God's mercy. He has brought me all that my heart desires. Say yes."

Lucy came flying into the room and grabbed his arm as she grinned at him. "I heard you, Johnjohn. Did you miss me?"

Megan was close behind her sister and grabbed his other arm. "Can we go home, please? I think the kitties are missing me."

He rose to his feet, lifting both girls in his arms. "I

have missed you both and your mother most of all. What do you say, Willa? May we go home now?"

"Yes."

"Will you marry me? With these two witnesses, will you promise to love and cherish me for as long as we both shall live?"

Willa drew a deep breath and rose to her feet. "Yes."

She raised her face for his kiss and her daughters squealed in delight.

After two nerve-racking days without hearing from the sheriff, Willa started to relax. Perhaps Miriam didn't know Willa was the woman her husband had been looking for. Debra left a message on the machine at the phone hut, telling them her friend was willing to take their case at no cost and would be out to see them after the first of the year but to call if they needed her before then.

John spoke to the bishop and made plans to marry her on the Tuesday after Christmas. She could barely believe John was willing to wed her after all he had learned, but he constantly reassured her that he was.

On the morning of the third day, Willa was filling the coffeepot with water when she looked out the kitchen window and saw a white SUV with the county sheriff's logo printed on the side. It pulled to a stop in front of the house. A second unmarked black car stopped behind it. Her newfound faith in God's mercy was about to be put to the test.

John moved to stand behind her and laid his hands on her shoulders. "I know Sheriff Bradley. He is a *goot* man."

"But he must obey the law." It was too late to run. Where could she hide?

"We must have faith in God's goodness."

"That's easy for you to say. They aren't your children."

He turned Willa around to face him. "Those words are painful to hear. I love the girls as if they were my own. To see them taken away from us would break my heart into tiny pieces. The will of God can be difficult to accept, but even in our sorrow He is with us. This is our faith."

She wrapped her arms around him. "I'm sorry. Forgive me. I'm afraid."

"I know you are, but I have seen you be very brave for the sake of your children. Be brave now."

Vera came into the room. "Did I hear a car?" At Willa's nod, she said, "I'll keep the girls in their room until you send for them."

John led Willa to the front door, opened it and stepped outside still holding her hand. Nick Bradley and her cousin Miriam got out of the SUV.

"Good morning." The sheriff nodded at them.

"What brings you out this way, Nick?" John asked.

Miriam came around the vehicle to stand beside her husband, but her gaze was fixed on Willa. "Hello, cousin. We have brought Gary and Nora Chase with us. They have asked Nick to make a welfare check on their grandchildren. Are the girls here?"

Willa was trembling so hard she thought she might fall down. She couldn't speak. John slipped his arm around her shoulders and pulled her against his side. "They are. Come inside. It is too cold to stand out here and we have much to talk about."

The doors of the black car opened, and Willa got

her first look at her in-laws. They didn't look like evil people. The man bore a stunning resemblance to his deceased son. He had graying hair and wore glasses, but she would have known him as Glen's father anywhere. The woman with him was blonde and slightly plump. She gripped her husband's arm tightly. Willa saw an odd mixture of hope and fear cross her face as she looked up at him. He covered her hand with his own in a gesture of comfort.

Willa turned away and went inside. She could hear the girls laughing in their room. She wanted to fly to them and gather them into her arms.

Please, God, I trust You to be with them and with me whatever Your plan is for us, but don't destroy their happiness. They are so young and innocent.

She moved into the kitchen and sat in the rocker by the stove. She clasped her hands together. Her fingers were ice-cold. John stood by her side with his hand on her shoulder.

The sheriff and Miriam took seats at the table. Willa's in-laws remained standing awkwardly in the center of the room. Miriam said, "I don't believe you have met these people."

Willa raised her chin. "My husband wanted nothing to do with them."

Glen's mother turned to hide her face in her husband's shoulder. His arm went around her. He cleared his throat. "We are aware of our son's feelings. I assure you it was one-sided. We loved Glen. We only wanted to help him."

Willa hardened her heart. "You chased him away from every job, from every home we tried to make.

We lived in terror that you would find us and take our daughters away. How was that helping?"

Gary flinched but faced her. "Glen became a compulsive gambler as a teenager. It only got worse no matter how often we tried to help him. The break in our relationship came after my son stole a large amount of money from my business after I gave him a job there. I had no choice but to press charges. That's when he started running."

Willa bristled. "I never knew Glen to gamble."

Nora patted her husband's arm and faced Willa. "Our private investigator was often able to locate Glen by having the gambling windows watched at the larger racetracks."

Willa frowned. "He worked at the racetracks."

Gary nodded. "He did, but never for long because of his gambling."

Willa didn't want to believe him, but it explained so much: the large sums of money that disappeared quickly and the weeks without any pay. "You told him you were going to take the children away."

Nora stepped closer. "We were overjoyed when Glen called us to help with the babies after you became ill. We saw a chance to reconcile with our son. While you were hospitalized, I was home alone with the babies when a man Glen owed money to came to collect. It was so frightening. He left, but when Glen came home, Gary and I told him we wanted temporary custody of the children while he got help for his compulsive gambling addiction at an inpatient facility."

Gary moved to stand beside Nora. "We wanted to make sure both he and the girls were safe. Glen agreed and signed the papers, but before he went into treatment, he took the girls to visit you and disappeared. After we learned of his death, we continued looking for you because we want to help and because we love our granddaughters. We don't want to take them away from you."

Miriam leaned forward on the table. "It's true, Willa. Nick checked out their story."

Willa looked at them in disbelief. "Glen lied about everything."

"Not everything," Nora said. "He loved you and his daughters very much. May we see the girls?"

John said, "Come with me and I'll reintroduce you to Megan and Lucy. They will be delighted to have a new *mammi* and *daddi*, but first I must tell you that Willa and I plan to marry. I will raise Willa's children as my own."

Nick chuckled. "We heard the news from Debra and your new attorney early this morning. Nora and Gary had plenty of questions about having Amish grandchildren."

Miriam smiled at Willa. "Fortunately, we were able to answer most of those questions, since we have an Amish granddaughter, too. If your girls are anything like Hannah was at three, watch out."

Gary grasped his wife's hand. "We just want to be a part of their lives."

Glen had wronged his parents and lied to her, but she knew he had been genuinely afraid of losing the girls. She glanced at John. He nodded and said, "Perhaps you would like to spend Christmas with us so we can get to know each other."

Gary looked at his wife. "We'd love that."

"You should come to the school's Christmas program

tonight," Miriam suggested. "It will give you a feel for the kind of education your grandchildren will have."

"Plus, Hannah has a major part in the play they're putting on," Nick said with a knowing smile for his wife.

The girls were shy of their new grandparents at first, but by midafternoon they were showing Gary and Nora the kittens and cows in the barn and introducing them to the horses. John came into the house while they were exploring. Willa was washing dishes. "Are you all right?" he asked.

She sighed heavily. "All these years of fear for nothing. I still can't believe it. I was wrong to doubt God's mercy so long. I can't imagine how Nora and Gary must have suffered."

"We will make it up to them. Shall we take the sleigh or the buggy to the school program tonight?"

She touched a soapy finger to his nose. "I have a fondness for sleighs, as one brought us together."

"Fond enough to name our boy Melvin? It was his sleigh."

"I have always liked that name."

He rubbed his nose on her *kapp* and kissed her forehead. "Then the sleigh it is."

They attended the late performance. Vera was in her element as she explained their Amish customs and answered Nora's questions. Afterward, the family rode home slowly along the snow-covered country road as the brilliant stars came out overhead. The only sounds were the hissing of the runners over the snow and the jingle of harness bells. Willa snuggled against John and leaned her head on his shoulder. The peace of

Christmas Eve seeped into her heart and healed the wounds of Glen's betrayal.

God had brought a fine man into her life, and she was a fool if she didn't hold on to him.

When they reached home, Willa and Nora put the girls to bed and had to read only one story before the twins were both fast asleep.

John leaned back in his chair and glanced up as Nora and Willa came into the kitchen, where he and Gary had been enjoying a cup of coffee after having decorated the mantel and window ledges with pine boughs.

Willa drew a deep breath and smiled. "It smells wonderful in here."

Vera came in with several large candles and holders in her hands. "It finally seems like Christmas. Willa, will you place the candles in the windows so the world may see them shining brightly and know the light of the Christ child is found in this household?"

John's heart overflowed with love for Willa as he watched her place a candle in the kitchen window and light it. In a few more days she would be his wife. Suddenly, her face grew pale. Her knuckles turned white as her fingers tightened on the window ledge. He sprang to his feet. "What's wrong?"

Willa started panting. "It's time."

"Are you sure? Could this be false labor?" his mother asked.

"*Nee*, this is the real thing. My back has been aching for a while." She drew a deep breath and stood upright.

"It's too soon." Fear clutched John's chest.

Willa shook her head. "The midwife said this one might come early. My dates could be off."

His mother turned to him. "Fetch the midwife."

John felt as if his feet had turned to lead. Willa's baby was coming, and he wasn't yet her husband. "I will fetch the bishop, too."

"You don't have to, John," Willa said softly.

"I don't need to, but I want to." How much time did he have? "I'll hitch up the buggy."

Gary took John by the arm. "It will be faster if we use my car. It has four-wheel drive."

As the men rushed out the door, Nora took Willa by the arm. "Are you ready to lie down, or do you want to walk?"

"I'll walk. I hope they hurry."

They did. Willa was standing in the living room holding on to the fireplace mantel when John and Gary rushed in with a sleepy and slightly grumpy bishop.

"Where is the midwife?" Nora demanded, looking past them.

"I called her. She is on her way," Gary assured her.

Willa gritted her teeth as another contraction hit. "I hate to rush you, Bishop Beachy, but I don't think we have much time."

The flustered man motioned to John. "Take her hand. Maid of honor stand at Willa's side and the groomsman stand beside John."

Nora stepped back to allow Vera to stand beside Willa, but Willa shook her head and held out her hand. "Nora, I would be most pleased if you would stand up with me."

"Are you sure?"

"You are part of my family. I'm sure."

"Don't you need rings?" Gary asked, working his wedding band off.

"*Nee*, we do not use such worldly symbols," the bishop said kindly.

Willa grasped John's hand and felt him tremble. "Are you sure?" she whispered.

He squeezed her fingers as he smiled at her. "I am the happiest man on earth at this moment. I'm sure. Are you?"

Willa thought she knew exactly how he felt. "There is not a doubt in my heart."

Together they listened to the solemn words of the ceremony and answered "I do" in strong, sure voices.

The bishop raised his hand to bless them. "I pronounce you husband and wife and what *Gott* has joined together let no man put asunder."

The outside door opened, and Janice Willard came in with a large black bag. She paused as she saw the gathering. "What did I miss?"

"Not the most important part," John said. He turned to Willa, gently pulled her into his arms and kissed her. A second later another, stronger, contraction hit, and she bowed her head against his shoulder. She couldn't stifle the moan that rose to her throat.

"I know that sound," Janice said as she moved John out of the way and took Willa's arm. "Let's get you into bed."

In the early hours of Christmas morning, Melvin John Miller made his appearance in the world, and Willa wondered how so much pure love and joy could arrive in a six-pound-two-ounce bundle.

The twins were excited to find a new baby had arrived in the night, but they worried it might have to go back home later. Willa assured them baby Melvin was theirs to keep.

At John's suggestion, Gary invited the girls outside to see another gift. The sled John had made sat on the front porch. Megan and Lucy soon had Gary pulling them around the yard on it until he was red in the face. When he tired, Nora took over, laughing like a kid herself.

John sat on the edge of the bed beside Willa and gazed in awe at the child sleeping in her arms. "You have a beautiful son."

Willa looked tired but happy. "We have a beautiful son."

John reached out and drew his fingers along the curve of her cheek. "I have received a pair of *schnickelfritz*, a newborn son and a *frau* I love with all my heart as my Christmas gifts. I'm afraid I will wake and find it has all been a dream."

She captured his hand and pressed a kiss into his palm. "I am not a dream. I love you, husband, with all my heart."

"It was hard for me to believe in love again, but you and your children have convinced me that God wishes us to be a family." He leaned his forehead against hers and whispered, "I will never stop giving thanks for your love."

"I trust God to make our lives joyful. I trust that he will give us more children to love and years to work together side by side. I know we shall have obstacles to overcome and trials to endure, but I will do my best to make you a good wife."

John's lips touched hers with incredible gentleness, a featherlight touch. The sweet softness of his lips moved away from her mouth. He kissed her cheek and then her brow. It wasn't enough. She cupped his face with her hand and brought his mouth back to hers. To her delight, he deepened the kiss. Joy clutched her heart and stole her breath away.

Slowly, he drew back. Willa wasn't ready to let him go. She would never be ready.

"I love you, Willa," he murmured softly into her ear. "You made me whole again. I was brokenhearted and on the edge of despair. You and your beautiful daughters found a way to mend me."

"I lived a life ashamed of what I had done. I thought I was beyond help. I thought I didn't deserve the wonderful babies God had given me. And then you came into my life and I saw hope and I found faith."

He kissed her again and then leaned down to kiss the baby's head. There was a knock at her door. Gary and Nora came in with Vera and the twins. The girls edged close to the bed to admire their new brother.

"I like him," Megan said, touching him softly.

"I like him more," Lucy added, taking hold of his little hand. She looked at John. "Are you sure we can keep him?"

John smiled. "I'm sure."

"Are you our daddy now?" Megan asked.

He nodded solemnly. "*Ja*, I am your *daed*. Is this okay?"

Megan stared at him a long moment. "Does this mean we're your Amish daughters?"

"*Ja, Gott* has given me Amish Christmas twins as a gift. I love you and your little brother very much."

The girls climbed on the bed and put their arms around his neck. Lucy kissed his cheek. "We love you, too, Johnjohn."

In that moment, Willa thanked God for the mysteriously twisted path that had brought them all to this place. It was exactly where they belonged.

* * * * *

If you enjoyed AMISH CHRISTMAS TWINS,
look for the other books in the
AMISH BACHELORS *series:*

AN AMISH HARVEST
AN AMISH NOEL
HIS AMISH TEACHER
THEIR PRETEND AMISH COURTSHIP

And don't miss the next
CHRISTMAS TWINS *story,*
SECRET CHRISTMAS TWINS
by Lee Tobin McClain,
available November 2017!

Dear Reader,

First, I want to wish you a blessed Christmas season. Life brings us all unexpected joys and unexpected heartaches, but He is never far from us if we trust in His love and mercy.

The issue of postpartum psychosis is one that attracts attention only when a woman suffering from it does the unthinkable. My grandmother suffered from this illness, although it wasn't diagnosed as such back in those days. My aunt once told me that my grandfather had to tie a rope to his wife and take her with him into the fields where he worked because he feared she would hurt herself or the children while he was gone. Thankfully, only a very small number of women have such acute cases.

If you would like more information on this illness, I suggest you visit www.postpartum.net and click on the following link: Postpartum psychosis help and info.

There are countless women who have suffered with postpartum psychosis and recovered completely. The key is getting immediate help. If you suspect that someone you love has postpartum psychosis, she should not be alone at any time until a professional diagnosis is received and she is under the continuous care of a health-care provider.

Bringing awareness of this condition and the need for continuing research was my mission in writing this story. I wanted my grandmother's illness brought to light, not hidden as it was for so many years. She died before I had the chance to know her. In some small way, this story is my tribute to her.

I pray the holidays bring you many joys, and if you have a *schnickelfritz* or two in your life, give them a Christmas hug from me.

Blessings,

Patricia Davids

COMING NEXT MONTH FROM
Love Inspired®

Available October 17, 2017

SECRET CHRISTMAS TWINS
Christmas Twins • by Lee Tobin McClain

Erica Lindholm never expected her Christmas gift would be becoming guardian to twin babies! But fulfilling her promise to keep their parentage a secret becomes increasingly difficult when her holiday plans mean spending time with—and falling for—their uncle, Jason Stephanidis, on the family farm.

AN AMISH PROPOSAL
Amish Hearts • by Jo Ann Brown

Pregnant and without options, Katie Kay Lapp is grateful when past love Micah Stoltzfus helps her find a place to stay. But when he proposes a marriage of convenience, she refuses. Because Katie Kay wants much more—she wants the heart of the man she once let go.

CHRISTMAS ON THE RANCH
by Arlene James and Lois Richer

Spend Christmas with two handsome ranchers in these two brand-new holiday novellas, where a stranger's joyful spirit provides healing for one bachelor, and a single mom with a scarred past is charmed by her little girl's wish for a cowboy daddy.

THE COWBOY'S FAMILY CHRISTMAS
Cowboys of Cedar Ridge • by Carolyne Aarsen

Returning to the Bar W Ranch, Reuben Walsh finds his late brother's widow, Leanne, fighting to keep the place running. Reuben's committed to helping out while he's around—even if it means spending time with the woman who once broke his heart. Can they come to an agreement—and find a happily-ever-after in time for the holidays?

THE LAWMAN'S YULETIDE BABY
Grace Haven • by Ruth Logan Herne

Having a baby dropped on his doorstep changes everything for state trooper Gabe Cutter. After asking widowed single mom next door Corinne Gallagher for help, he's suddenly surrounded by the lights, music and holiday festivities he's avoided for years. This Christmas, can they put their troubled pasts behind and create a family together?

A TEXAS HOLIDAY REUNION
Texas Cowboys • by Shannon Taylor Vannatter

After his father volunteers Colson Kincaid to help at Resa McCall's ranch over Christmas, the single dad is reunited with his old love. Colson's used to managing horses, but can he keep his feelings for Resa from spilling over—and from revealing a truth about his daughter's parentage that could devastate them forever?

LICNM1017

Get 2 Free Books,
Plus 2 Free Gifts—
just for trying the Reader Service!

Love Inspired